Imelda

By the same author

Descent
A Truth Lover
Memoirs of my Aunt Minnie and Clapperton
Pagan's Pilgrimage
Stories Short and Tall
Voice Without Restraint: Bob Dylan's Lyrics and Their Background
Three Novellas
The Double in Nineteenth-Century Fiction

Imelda
and other stories

John Herdman

[signature: John Herdman]

Polygon
EDINBURGH

© John Herdman 1993

Published by Polygon
22 George Square
Edinburgh

Set in Garamond
by Alden Multimedia, Northampton

**Printed and bound in Great Britain by
Hartnolls Limited, Bodmin, Cornwall**

Herdman, John
Imelda and Other Stories
  I. Title
  823'. 914 [F]

ISBN 0 7486 6140 9

The Publisher acknowledges subsidy from the Scottish
Arts Council towards publication of this volume.

Acknowledgements

The Devil and Dr Tuberose was first published in Scotland in *Chapman* and in the U.S. in *Beloit Fiction Journal,* and was the title story of *Scottish Short Stories 1991* (Harper Collins). *The Day I Met the Queen Mother* was the title story of *New Writing Scotland 8* (Association for Scottish Literary Studies). *Fates, The Emperor Bolingbroke III, The Tweak* and *Dealing with a Bore* were broadcast on BBC Radio Scotland. *Original Sin* appeared in *Chapman, Acquainted with Grief* in the *Glasgow Herald, Fates* in *Our Duncan, who art in Trent. . .* (Harris Press), and *The Emperor Bolingbroke III, The Tweak* and *Dealing with a Bore* in *Words.*

Contents

Imelda

Increpasti superbos;
  maledicti qui errant a praeceptis tuis.

Psalmus 118, III Ghimel
(Psalterium Monasticum)

7/35 Burnside Quadrant,
Bellshill,
Lanarkshire

26 April 1986

Dear Major Agnew,

I hope you will forgive me writing to you out of the blue. My parents, Mr and Mrs Dan Johnstone who used to live in Berwickshire, were given your name and address by a friend Mrs Lambie who stays near you. My Dad at one time used to work on the Lemington estate as a tractorman, but we moved here in 1964.

I was adopted when I was two months old, and ever since my parents told me about it when I was twelve, there has never been any secret that I belonged to the Agnew family of Lemington. I believe my father's name was Hubert Agnew and my mother was Imelda Cranstoun. They were engaged to be married but my father died shortly before I was born and that is why I was adopted. Now that I am married myself and soon to be a mother, I would really like to know more about my original family and if possible make contact with my real mother. Mrs Lambie thought that you would be the person who would know most about the family.

I worked as a nurse until recently and my husband David is in computers. I do hope that I am not intruding on your privacy by writing to you like this, if you feel I am being cheeky please just ignore my letter.

Yours sincerely,

Janice Moodie (Mrs)

Fingleton Den Cottage,
Lemington
Berwickshire

30 April 1986

Dear Mrs Moodie,

How very pleased I was to receive your letter. Needless to say I was aware of your existence, but I knew nothing of your present whereabouts, and it is better, I always feel, not to pry into these things, and rather to let life take its own course until something happens to make one act otherwise. I am looking at it from my own end of the wicket, of course: I fully understand why you should wish at this time to learn something of your true background, and I am only too happy to be of any assistance to you, though what I can offer by way of direct information is limited.

As to your main line of enquiry, the possibility of making contact with your mother, I had best not beat about the bush. I am sorry to have to tell you that your mother died in London in 1981. I know very little about the circumstances. I must explain that most of my life has been spent far from Berwickshire as my career was that of a professional soldier, and my contact with the family during those years were tenuous. I retired at the age of fifty in 1980 and returned to Berwickshire, since when I have been taking a considerable interest in family history and family affairs– one of those interests that grows on one as one gets older and has time on one's hands. I am first cousin to your late father, being of the cadet branch of the family although quite a number of years older than Hubert, my uncle (your grandfather) having married comparatively late in life.

Although I have very little personal, first-hand knowledge of your parents' youth and the circumstances surrounding your birth, I have in my possession two extraordinary documents relating to those years, photocopies of which I am sending to you herewith. The first was written by your uncle Frank, your father's younger brother, of whom you probably know nothing. He is, I am afraid, a paranoid schizophrenic, and has been a patient at the Royal Edinburgh Hospital ever since suffering a complete mental breakdown early in 1963. He sent this autobiographical essay, if that is the right term for it, to me five years ago in response to the news of your mother's death, which it had been my sad duty to communicate to him by letter.

Frank lives in a little world of his own, as you will see when you read the piece, and his motives in writing it and sending it to me are best known to himself. But he is not *completely* crazy; indeed they let him out of hospital sometimes, on probation as it were; but he feels highly insecure in the outside world and always quickly becomes sufficiently unwell again to be able to retreat once more within the protecting walls. As a nurse, you will no doubt understand. The story he tells is so amazing, both in style and in content, and in many respects so inherently improbable, that I felt I really must try to have some light cast on the whole business from some more balanced and objective source. Accordingly I made contact with the sole surviving independent witness of the events related in Frank's narrative, Sir Robert Affleck. Sir Robert was the brother of Hubert and Frank's mother, and a cousin of Imelda's mother. When Imelda was orphaned he became her guardian, and in the early 1950s came to live with her at Lemington. That is how Hubert, Frank and your mother came to be brought up together.

At the time when Frank's memoir reached me, Sir Robert was living in an old people's home in Kelso. Although well over eighty he still had his wits very much about him. Without any mention whatever of Frank, whom Sir Robert had not seen for eighteen years, I asked the old man to furnish me with an account of the Agnew family during the years when he lived at Lemington. I did not want him to be *replying* to Frank, or refuting the version of events provided by that unfortunate individual, I wanted his own unbiased recollections (if such a thing is ever possible). He knew of my interest in family history and my request seemed to him in no way odd; he responded readily and promptly. It is as well that I asked him when I did, for writing that account was the old fellow's last significant act on earth. Two days after sending me his memoir he died of a massive apoplectic seizure—or stroke, as I believe you medical people call it nowadays.

These, then, are the two documents which I am sending to you. As you will see, they are astonishingly different, sometimes in direct contradiction to each other, yet in some odd unexpected ways they confirm and complement each other too. There is absolutely no one left alive whom one could ask to adjudicate between them, unless indeed Johnny Restorick, Sir Robert's body servant, be still living and even if he is, adjudication would scarcely be his forte. Johnny Restorick disappeared utterly without trace soon after the events described in these narratives, and nothing has ever been seen or heard of him since. So you must make of this story what you can. It is a most dark and melancholy tale, and I only hope that it will not upset you too much.

I am also sending you—registered and under separate cover—some family photographs which I should be most grateful if you could return to me as they cannot be replaced. They show your parents and grandparents, your Uncle Frank, and Uncle Affleck (as Sir Robert was always known in the family) at different times in their lives. I hope that after perusing all this material you will still feel happy to be an Agnew. Ours is a proud and an ancient race, and as I am unmarried and likely to remain so, you may soon be its sole surviving representative. Should you ever have occasion to be in Berwickshire, you and your husband would be more than welcome to visit me here in my little retreat. Lemington, of course, is now Lemington Country House Hotel.
With every good wish,
Yours sincerely,

Rufus G. Agnew

Memoir Of Frank Agnew, Otherwise Known As Superbo

I

Imelda, Imelda, are you truly gone from us, beautiful bright angel? In what Elysian fields do you now walk? For you have I scaled the heights of folly, descended into the abyss of madness and self-alienation, struggled in the maelstrom of despair. I rave, you say ... but what else, pray, can a poor madman do? Is not raving our vocation? Whom am I addressing, out of my heart's loneliness and desolation? No longer Imelda, surely, for she is gone ... Enough, enough. Rhetoric, farewell.

I can scarcely remember a time before Imelda. The floods of 12th August, 1948: those, certainly, I recall. The Fintrace Burn turned into a mighty roaring torrent, the Whitadder into a swelling ocean: the haughs became spacious lakes, great trees islanded, the plain of the Merse transformed into the likeness of a Louisiana bayou. My father took us out in his new Austin to see the devastation, my brother and me. For myself, the broken bridges and the ruined steadings recalled the fallen towers of Ilium, but Hubert could think of nothing but German bombing raids and busted dams. I can see the two of us now, I lost in the speechless wonder of a childhood almost quiveringly sensitive and alert, he a thickset, diffusely freckled redhead who might have been swinging from a tree, stotting around like a cretin, making booming and swooshing noises, trying to pretend that his right hand was an aeroplane, an exercise quite evidently preordained to failure.

I was just seven at the time, mark you, and he eight and a half. He was always obsessed with aeroplanes and air battles, and hoped for nothing more than the day when he could join the RAF for his National Service—it was a bitter disappointment to him when that prospect faded. He even insisted on calling our bulldog 'Wing Commander'. A little later in our childhood he began making model aircraft with balsa wood. I can still catch in the nostrils of memory the sharp, odious stench of the cement he used, and hear his heavy grunts of concentration as he struggled to make his stubby, clumsy fingers obey his will, for he had little manual dexterity. The finished articles were always imperfectly executed, stained with smears of dried cement, and I remember with peculiar aversion their obscene lightness and insubstantiality. On one occasion I deliberately smashed one of them, out of sheer disgust; I pretended that in pulling out a volume of the *Children's Encyclopaedia* from a shelf above the table where the model lay, I had inadvertently dislodged its companion which had fallen on the treasured achievement. I can still see the big silent tears running down either side of Hubert's nose among the freckles. The model had cost him four weeks of labour.

The eloquent contrast between the two of us is the main impression which I retain from our early childhood years. In those days quests for the Yeti, or Abominable Snowman, were all the rage, and I, mischievous and precocious urchin that I was, once suggested to my parents that they keep our dear Hubert safely within doors, lest he be carried off as a prize by some expedition to the Himalayas that might have strayed off course. I received a mild rebuke. As to our parents, they were mere ciphers. My father, who had inherited the Lemington estate shortly after his marriage at the age of forty, was wholly unequipped for the role of country gentleman. A retiring antiquarian who had never done a day's real work in his life, he now received a late vocation to the Epicopalian priesthood, and after ordination became rector of a small church a few miles away which had old associations with our family. At this point he called upon my mother's brother, Sir Robert Affleck, at that time factor of a large estate in the West Highlands, to take over the management of Lemington. The year was 1950. With Uncle Affleck came his ward, our second cousin Imelda.

It was a Saturday afternoon in September when they arrived. I was to leave in a few days' time for my first term at boarding school. My mother called me into the great drawing-room which looked across the broad lawn and the gorge beyond towards the distant Cheviot. 'This, Frank, is your Uncle Affleck, and this your cousin Imelda.' Standing before me with his back to the fireplace was a big man with a commanding presence, high-coloured and vigorous, with a prominent nose, a steady eye and a thick reddish moustache flecked with grey, dressed in a well-worn checked tweed jacket and baggy fawn corduroys. Holding his hand was a girl of about my own age. She was thin and pale-faced, her hair dark, parted at the centre and pulled back in a single long pigtail reaching to her waist. Shy, biting her lower lip, she was dressed in a thin cardigan and a short cotton print dress patterned with, I believe, forget-me-nots. Forget you I will not, Imelda! Never, while the sands of time shall run! We stood and gazed at each other, now; but it was curiosity, not yet love. She was wearing a little necklace with a blood-red stone. Her eyes were large and grey and soft, the eyes of a dove. How often were those eyes to gaze at me in years to come, and with what huge import! But now it was curiosity, on both our parts, curiosity and, of course, fear. For her it was a threatening new world, for me a worrying disturbance of the old. Already Hubert was hanging about heavily in her vicinity, trying without success to interest her in a balsa-wood Messerschmidt. It was a moment heavy with fate.

I do not remember Imelda speaking that first weekend, though I suppose she must have done. With ponderous good will Hubert set about *showing* her things, and willy-nilly she followed in his wake, having as yet no ground of her own on which to take a stand at Lemington; but from time to time she gazed at me as if beseeching rescue, as if I were the door through which she might escape to a truer and perhaps a more familiar world . . . . In those first hours, though, I somehow resented her presence. About to leave home for the first time, I wanted to remember it as it had always been, and here now were Imelda and Uncle Affleck changing it all, altering everything, reshaping my world so that its old dimensions were already gone for ever . . . Yet when I returned, at Christmas, it was as if I had never known Lemington without Imelda.

When Uncle Affleck took up residence at Lemington, Imelda had already been with him for a year. Her father, a Church of

Scotland missionary, had died in Africa from the bite of a venomous snake, and her sorrowing mother had been carried off a few months later by a tropical fever. My mother and Uncle Affleck were her mother's first cousins, and her nearest relatives. Sir Robert went out to Africa to bring her home, and took her back with him to the West Highlands. His devotion to her well-being was unlimited. A confirmed bachelor, he was deeply conscious of Imelda's need of motherly care, and for this reason he accepted the more readily my father's invitation that he should come to Lemington to manage our estate.

On his arrival Uncle Affleck tacitly assumed, as if by right, the headship of the household. All practical matters were in his hands. My father, overshadowed by a personality infinitely stronger and more decisive than his own, retreated into his study with a kind of cowed relief, and immersed himself in his fragile, allusive sermons and in his never-ending labours on the Third Statistical Account of our parish. My mother, fulfilled at last in the presence of a *real* man about the house, took on a new lease of life, openly idolised her brother and deferred to him in all things. Henceforth it was Uncle Affleck in whose hands the future of the house of Agnew was entrusted.

Imelda was not the only newcomer to arrive at Lemington in the train of Uncle Affleck. I was not aware of the presence of this other person in September; perhaps he arrived after I had departed for the school term. One morning not long after my return for the Christmas holidays I wandered dreamily into the stables, where I liked to skulk about by myself, lost in romantic imaginings. Turning a dark corner, I leapt involuntarily into the air and then froze with horror. Stooping over a pile of old hay in the shadow was a man in what I suppose was an old Army greatcoat, though it appeared to have been dyed a kind of mottled navy blue. He was extremely swarthy, suggesting almost a lick of the tarbrush, and had damp, greasy-looking, curly black hair. His face was bony and somehow asymmetrical, and several front teeth were missing. As he heard my gasp of fright he swung round with a sharp, furtive look, as if caught in some dubious act, but quickly relaxed, straightened up, and stood regarding me with his arms folded. He grinned, but I have never seen a smile less reassuring. There was a slight cast in one of his eyes. I backed away from him a few paces, but found myself unable to turn and flee: I stood as if hypnotised by a viper. Neither of us spoke. After some time had passed I became quite conscious that the man was wilfully torturing me. Then quite suddenly he unfolded his arms, and thrust within a few inches of my face the black stump of an arm, cut off above the wrist! Even in that dim half light I was preternaturally aware of an odd wrinkle, or pucker, on the very tip of its obscene roundness. He bent down towards me, still grinning.

'What d'ye think of that, eh?' he asked roughly. 'What d'ye think of *that*?'

This individual, from whom I now found the will to absent myself with marvellous rapidity, was, as I soon discovered, Johnny Restorick, my uncle's ex-batman. He was supposed to be a tinker, though his appearance suggested rather a Romany gipsy. He spoke in an accent that might have been Highland or might have been Irish, but did not seem to be quite either. The next time I saw him a metal hook was strapped onto his wrist with leather thongs, and, strangely enough, I never saw him without it again. He performed odd duties about the estate, none of them very essential, but always accompanied my uncle on his rounds, dogging him like a shadow. They seldom seemed to speak to each other but operated as a unit, Restorick carrying out my uncle's every order almost, it seemed, without having to be asked. I soon got to know Johnny in the ordinary course of events and in general found him, though taciturn in manner and cynical in attitude, to be not unfriendly, and certainly not actively hostile, to myself. The occasion of our first encounter was never referred to by either of us.

My relations with Uncle Affleck were complex. Growing up as I had done thus far, effectively fatherless–for my dreamy father was a will o' the wisp rather than a man–I no doubt looked up to Sir Robert and wordlessly asked him to fill that silently abdicated role. I found his aura of robust angularity singularly attractive, I admired his decisiveness, strove within myself to emulate his effortless mastery of the affairs of men. For his part he appeared to regard me with a detached, almost amused interest. I think he found me—as he could scarcely have failed to do—a vastly more stimulating companion than Hubert, my precocity of intellect and my rapidly developing good looks fascinated him, and by natural inclination he would beyond doubt have favoured me far above my brother.

But Uncle Affleck was a man of iron rectitude and a tremendously developed sense of family honour and duty. Hubert, dull knave though he was, was nonetheless the elder son, and heir to Lemington. It was Uncle Affleck's duty to nurture him, to try on him the alchemist's art, to change, it might be, his base metal into something even a little more like gold. It was a challenge which appealed, I do not doubt, to his imperious nature, his hunger to impress the seal of his will on the malleable wax of human affairs. As I grew older, I could not avoid realising that he had taken Hubert peculiarly under his protective wing. With the generosity of character innate in my disposition, I successfully effaced all traces of jealousy; until, that is, a terrible truth began to be relentlessly borne in upon me. As we grew into adolescence—and my brother, you will remember, was my senior by a year and a half—it became inescapably clear to me that Uncle Affleck intended Imelda for Hubert.

Understand, please, that I would have regarded that prospect with horror and outrage even had I myself felt nothing at all for Imelda. To think of subjecting a delicate, opening flower to the embrace of such as him ... I cannot ... Let me explain, let me describe ... No, not yet. I am anticipating. Forgive me. An ineluctable train of thought had carried me away. Let us return to childhood.

By the time Hubert and I came home from school that first Christmas, Imelda had grown accustomed to Lemington and had lost a little of her shyness. She still spoke little, it is true, but she followed the two of us about leech-like as we vied in introducing her to the damp leafy paths and the stagnant, weed-infested ponds, the treacherous neuks and crannies in the gorge, slippy with ice at that season, the curious hollow rock formations into which a child might squeeze and skulk unseen. Ironically, her arrival brought Hubert and myself into one another's company in a way that neither of us had ever sought or desired, and that simply because neither of us would willingly be out of her presence. Previously, we had led utterly unrelated lives, kept apart less by the insignificant divide which separated our ages than by the temperamental and intellectual gulf which yawned between us. In development of mind and soul, in everything that pertained to the inner life and the finer things of the spirit, it was Hubert who was still the unformed child, whereas I trembled on the verge of adult mysteries. In my brother, however, the purely animal instincts were already rampant. He assumed, in relation to Imelda, a role which even to my child's eye appeared an offensive parody of the dominant male role; and in doing so he effectively pushed me into the background, asserted—without, it must be said, a trace of malice—my irrelevance. When we had to climb a fence, scramble down a tricky slope, pick our way over a boggy patch, it was the Yeti who assisted Imelda, offered her his hand, affected a manly courage which made light of risk and danger. It was Hubert who explained things, who decided what was to be done that day, who answered to Uncle Affleck for Imelda's safety. Imelda was compliant to his dominance, welcomed it even, yet always she would look back to make sure that I was following, would wait for me to catch up, seek in some touching little way to include me—would take pains to ensure, in short, that we continued a threesome. And often I thought I read in her wistful gaze an insatiable regret that it was not *I* who was the elder, not *I* who could assume the right to take her hand with such confidence and assurance to lead her out of the path of danger.

For me, Imelda's presence was imbued with the spirit of the Africa whence she had come. She carried with her the mystery and glamour of far-off and exotic places. I seemed to sense in her a wayward, alien nature that came out of an earlier, more instinctual, less conscious world ... Oh yes, I felt all of this, young though I was, though I did not yet have the words in which to name it to myself and had never read D.H. Lawrence. In Imelda, gentle and wistful and sad-eyed though she was, I think I felt a dangerous, untamed spirit, something that bodied ill, that spoke of pain and sorrow to come. This *aperçu* was oddly associated for me with a certain physical circumstance. Imelda, when she came to us and indeed for years afterwards, was a bedwetter, and occasionally, when one was near her, one caught a delicate but definite scent of urine. This did not repel me—on the contrary in a curious way it actually added to her fascination. It was as if it connected her with the warm animal world of the estate, of byre and stable and stye, and beyond that, with the untrained, untamed force of nature ... Yes, Imelda was a defenceless, vulnerable but terrible force of nature, and that is a combination of adjectives that bodes no good.

Already in those early holidays, Hubert sometimes contrived to spirit Imelda away on expeditions from which I was excluded. Though thoroughly stupid, he had a foxy cunning that went well with his red hair, and he exploited the natural solitariness of my nature, my tendency to wander off by myself on occasion without giving a thought to the possible consequences, to steal a march on me in a rivalry that within a year or two was becoming conscious for both of us. It was probably on one such occasion that, in some curious spirit of perversity, I decided to cultivate the acquaintance of Johnny Restorick. After our first inauspicious meeting, strangely, I had lost all fear of him, as if the horror that was inherent in his appearance and personality had been revealed to me all in one instant, had been instantaneously accepted and no longer exercised any hold over me. For mystic terror lies not in what we know but in what we fear may be disclosed, and I had swallowed the truth of Restorick in a single gulp. I knew beyond doubting, as I stood there facing him in the stable, that there was no evil of which he was not capable. I now experienced an urge to become *privy* to him, if I may express it thus. I did not wish to become evil like him, but I wanted to plumb his depths, to understand in a more conscious way what and why he was. In this I was partly motivated by my rivalry with Hubert. Hubert would never have admitted to fear of Restorick, but I saw how he avoided him, how he dropped his eyes, almost in *embarrassment* when the tinker was about, and busied himself with some little task or preoccupation in order to cover up his discomfiture. My own self-respect in face of the *fact* of Restorick somehow gave me an edge over Hubert, opened up a potential area in which I might have the advantage of him.

As for Imelda, the figure of Uncle Affleck's ex-batman inspired her with unconcealed terror. She shrank away from him, retreated behind Hubert or myself, sometimes actually hid when she saw him coming; she turned paler, if that is possible, and her breath came faster. His appearance alone, frightening though it was, did not seem to be enough to account for it. Restorick had been with Uncle Affleck when she first lived with him in the West Highlands, of course, and I often wondered whether she possessed some dark knowledge about him or his past to arouse such extreme displays of recoil. Looking back at those days, I think that it was rather presentiment than memory. Already Restorick was casting his dark shadow on the future of us all, and Imelda, child of nature, tuned in to the subtle reality of coming evil, could already see the approaching cloud.

So it may have been with some idea of impressing Imelda as well as Hubert with my intrepidity, and of cocking a snook at both of them for their exclusion of me, that one day I began, wordlessly, to dog the heels of Restorick as he went about his business. I was fascinated by his dexterity with the hook. He was mending fences that first day, I remember, and he tolerated my presence without comment, only sometimes pausing in his work to favour me with a twisted, knowing but not unfriendly grin. He seemed to feel that he had acquired a protégé, almost made a conquest, and for me it was enough to be accepted, and to tread on a path on which Hubert would never follow me or usurp my rights. With Restorick I began to have a friendship of silence, a silence which implied complicity, though that complicity was utterly without content. It was as yet mere *form*, awaiting the fateful moment when it would be filled up and bodied forth.

Restorick, I soon learned, had one special field of knowledge and expertise. He had an astonishing knowledge of the natural properties of herbs and plants, both medicinal and toxic and an even greater store of learning on the subject of fungi. It was, I suppose, part of the traditional lore of the travelling folk from whom he was reputed to come: his clan, it was said, belonged to the far north, to Orkney and Caithness and Sutherland. When Johnny saw that I was interested in the occasional remarks he would make on the subject of herbs and fungi, he began to take me into the woods and fields of the estate in search of beautiful or unusual specimens: I became totally absorbed in this pursuit. Herbs held only a limited interest for me, but in fungi I took an almost sensuous pleasure and delight. I acquired the *Observer's Book of British Fungi* and always carried it with me on our expeditions. Johnny did not know the scientific names, of course, but that was all that he did not know.

'Here's a boy that could kill a man,' he remarked casually one time, bending down and encircling a fine red and white-spotted specimen protectively, almost lovingly, with his hook.

'Would it kill him quickly or slowly, Johnny?' I asked breathlessly.

He gave me an unpleasant, twisted grin. 'Juist as fast or as slow as ye liked,' he replied, and did not elaborate.

Another time he indicated an insignificant-looking brownish toadstool.

'That fellae could mak a young chap gae mad,' he whispered, 'nae bother. You want tae watch that fellae.'

Restorick had an excuse for going on fungus-hunting excursions, for he supplied the cook with mushrooms at appropriate seasons. I am sure that he had some kind of liaison with the surly-looking woman; at any rate he was always hanging about the kitchen. I could plead no such justification, however, and it became very plain that Uncle Affleck disapproved in the highest degree of my association with his ex-batman. He was, I know, justified, for the tinker was a wholly unsuitable companion for a growing boy but in spite of my admiration for my uncle I resented his assumption of a quasi-parental authority. He also, of course, tried to keep me away from Imelda, for as we entered our teens it came increasingly plain that Uncle Affleck's dynastic intentions for his ward and Hubert were ever in the forefront of his mind. He took his duties as guardian extremely seriously, and was almost obsessively concerned for Imelda's happiness and well-being, and absurdly over-protective.

But indeed, everyone in our household loved Imelda. The only person who sometimes exhibited a strange kind of resentment of her was my mother. On one occasion at dinner, I remember, Imelda gently disagreed with her about some trifling matter.

'That's quite enough lip out of you, little Miss Pissabed,' was her outrageous response.

Imelda blushed scarlet and hung her head in a shame awful to behold, and all present—my father, myself, and even the insentient Hubert—were shocked to the marrow. My mother would never have dared, of course, to utter these words in front of Uncle Affleck. It was out of character; in fact, I had the distinct impression—so sensitive was I already in my psychological perception—that her outburst was actually occasioned by jealousy of Imelda because of the attention her brother paid to the girl's welfare. My mother worshipped the very ground Sir Robert stood on, never quarrelled with one of his opinions, and permitted him to exercise an unlimited ascendancy over her husband, and to usurp his proper functions in the household. As to my father, he was scarcely aware of anything that went on outside his study walls. He had his sermons to write, and work on the Third Statistical Account of Lemington Parish was always going slowly.

By the time he had reached his mid-teens, the Yeti had grown into a great, slobbering lout. As Arthur Balfour once said of a fellow politician, 'A little more brains and he would have been half-witted.' A great umbrella of coarse, uneven, reddish hair stood out from his forehead, like a parasol whose edges had been chewed by a rat; it overhung a face which might have arisen from some primeval swamp. He could talk of nothing but aeroplanes, dog-fights and bombing raids, and he farted incessantly, day and night. As a child he had gorged himself ceaselessly on fries, Mars Bars, crisps and ice cream, and at sixteen his digestion was already ruined. So awful was the impression that he made, that our father, gentle and dreamy creature that he was, had been known to wonder aloud whether Hubert were really his; one glance at my mother would have disabused him of this suspicion, but he never glanced at her, so he could not know.

Was it possible that the tender, delicate Imelda could prefer this monster to myself? As the years passed, it seemed, on the surface, increasingly likely that this unbelievable was the truth. As if by an ineluctable decree of fate, she was with him more and more, and I was progressively edged into the background. I speak of course of the school holidays, for both Hubert and myself were absent at boarding-school for the greater part of the year. Imelda however had been kept at home by Uncle Affleck's possessive protective-ness, shielded and insulated and cocooned from the outside world, educated by visiting teachers and tutors, by my father, and by Uncle Affleck himself. There was no doubt in my mind that she was being brainwashed into regarding Hubert as her destined mate, and that out of duty, loyalty and gratitude to Uncle Affleck she was wilfully doing violence to her own nature. I observed that she was now sometimes harsh and dismissive with me, looked away when I came into the room, and forced herself to speak to Hubert about things that could have held no real interest for her, when it would have been far more natural to converse with me on the thousand and one topics in which we both delighted. All these signs spoke not of aversion to me, but of the reverse. Imelda was trying to turn herself into something she was not, and this involved also the attempt to see in Hubert someone who was most assuredly not there.

This process was assisted by a very odd metamorphosis under-gone by the Yeti during his last year at school. In the first place he brushed his hair back, making an end of the umbrella, took to smoking a pipe, and sometimes even sported a bow-tie. Then he suddenly lost all interest in aeroplanes and started prattling instead about German metaphysics. Where before his talk had been all of Sopwith Pups, Tiger Moths, Junkers and Messerschmidts, now we heard nothing from him but epistemologies and categorical imperatives. This sea-change coincided with the ending of National Service, and perhaps, cheated of the prospect of two years on the wing, Hubert sought solace in the airy flights of philosophy. True, he spoke for a time of making his career in the RAF, but Uncle Affleck would not hear of this, no doubt because this choice would have kept him away from Imelda for far too long.

So now, incredible though it must seem, everyone suddenly came to regard Hubert as an intellectual. Some people appear to imagine that a young man has only to brush his hair back and to start smoking a pipe and talking about Leibnitz to be transformed overnight from a clown into a genius. Hubert's intellectual stature was immediately and quite uncritically accepted. They even managed to obtain for him entrance to the University of St. Andrews, a place, admittedly, where dunderheads from public schools are always welcome.

There could be only one explanation for all this. Uncle Affleck had realised that the Yeti's suit would stand no chance unless he transformed his appearance, his manner, and his overt interests. Accordingly he had been instructed to pull his socks up, and to step into a new personality specially rigged up for him by Uncle Affleck. Philosophy and Hubert were as ill-matched as Hubert and Imelda; but the Yeti was by nature a biddable creature, and possessed a certain malleable, chameleon-like ability to put on an attitude or a set of opinions like a suit of clothes, to make the right noises and even say the right words, without being capable of arriving at the very least inwardness with the position he was taking up; and there are plenty of people—the great majority, in fact—who will be perfectly satisfied with such a counterfeit. Imelda was not one of these; but on the other hand, the human capacity for wilful self-deception is almost limitless, and the pressures on the poor girl to conform to Uncle Affleck's will must have seemed well-nigh irresistible. As to myself, I had by now ceased to be a mere nuisance to my uncle, and had become a serious threat to his dynastic ambitions.

It must be appreciated that in those days I was a truly magnificent creature. Imagine one in the full strength of young manhood, with chiselled, almost hawk-like features, a flawless complexion, sleek, wavy, raven hair with a glossy sheen upon it bespeaking health and youthful vigour. My blue eye, clear and keen as the sky of a northern morning, was bold and frank, but with just a touch of imperiousness, an innate quality of command which would brook no trifling. My brow was lofty and fine, my jaw and the lines of my mouth exquisitely modelled, at once sensitive and assured, and with a provocative hint of sensuality in the proud curve of the lips. I was always in the van of fashion, but there was, too, a certain haughty negligence about my attire; and I carried myself with the natural ease and grace that is a stranger to artifice. Add to all this a beautifully modulated light baritone speaking voice, candid and mellifluous, and you will own that I must have made an impression not readily forgotten.

Allied to my physical graces and distinction of bearing were exceptional qualities of mind. There was no philosophical problem so abstruse but it was at once transparently open to the pellucid clarity of my intellect. Hubert's slow, ponderous conjectures and grunting labours–those of a 'metaphysical Bustard', in Coleridge's apt phrase–must yield at once to the elegant yet penetrating strokes of my mental razor, probing relentlessly and with infallible precision to the very root of the matter in hand. My conclusions, again, were formulated with an elegant lucidity which appeared, and in fact generally was, effortless. In human affairs I was no less incisive. My knowledge of the human heart was deep and instinctual, the delicacy of my perceptions fortified by the precision and justice of my critical faculties. While my intellect could lay no claim to architectonic massiveness, nor as yet had I great breadth of learning, yet there was a fundamental strength, sanity and clear-sightedness in my judgement which lent to my conceptions an unusual largeness and freedom.

Yet to all of these exceptional endowments and recommendations Imelda seemed oddly impervious. Did she find in my bearing, perhaps, a hint of displeasing arrogance? For, to tell the truth, it was impossible for me to be wholly unconscious of my powers and advantages. Imelda often referred to me as 'Superbo', and at times I wondered if there might not be a strain of intended satire in this just designation. However that might be, it was clear enough that Hubert's new personality had been devised specifically with an eye to meeting the threat posed to Uncle Affleck's plans by the undeniably powerful nature of my own appeal. In the nature of things it was a ploy inevitably doomed to failure, but it did not fail without in the process bringing horror and irremediable disaster on the house of Agnew.

II

It was near the beginning of the second year of Hubert's absence at university, and my first year away from school. I was at home at Lemington, totally immersed in the study of fungi, when, that is, I was not too aroused by my passion for Imelda to attend to anything at all. By rights, of course, I should have been a university freshman, for such was my intellectual distinction that no other course was imaginable to my parents than that I should tread the path of academic honours. But for the moment at least, I had set my face against such a plan. I had already embarked on my monumental study of *The Fungi of Berwickshire* and I claimed with justice that it was impossible for me to absent myself from the scene of my necessary fieldwork. I was making fairly frequent trips to Edinburgh to pursue the theoretical aspects of my calling, and so far had I already advanced in scientific method that I stood in no need of a tutor–unless it were Johnny Restorick, who could still teach me much from his vast store of traditional lore.

To tell the truth, however, I had a more compelling motive than toadstools for remaining at Lemington: I was quite determined to avail myself of the Yeti's absence at St. Andrews to displace him for ever in Imelda's affections. It was a heaven-sent opportunity, and one that would in all likelihood never come again. My parents remonstrated feebly, and Uncle Affleck made vigorous noises of protest and disgust, reiterating with wearisome predictability that I 'never did a hand's turn', that it was 'high time I did an honest day's work', that I should be 'black-burning ashamed' of my 'disgraceful idleness' and so on; and generally giving an airing to the traditional array of clichés appropriate to the circumstance. There are few forces so powerful as that of inertia, however. It is no easy matter to shift a young gentleman determined to stay put, even in the best-regulated families; and in our station of life it was not a viable option simply to turf a son out of the house–even a younger son–unceremoniously out on his ear. So I kept my head down and stood my ground, and when anyone asked what I was doing my mother would say, 'Oh, he's writing the most *marvellous* book about funguses–he's brilliant, you know.'

At first, whenever I tried to move in the direction of any intimacy with Imelda–by coming up close to her, asking her her thoughts, speaking of anything at all that seemed charged with an emotion which we might share–she pulled away from me, casting her eyes down, busying herself with some little task, hunching herself over a book, or in some way making light of any seriousness which I essayed. Out of doors, she plainly avoided me. I longed to walk with her among the haunts of our childhood, to let the eloquence of those scenes plead for me, remind her of the time when an unspoken but fragrant sympathy first arose between us. But she made sure that such an opportunity never occurred. Uncle Affleck was at the back of it, I knew; but with what weapons could I counter his inimical influence? I may say that I never ceased to admire Uncle Affleck, and even respected his motives, which essentially had to do with impersonal matters of family policy; while I was aware that his concern lest I displace his protégé Hubert in his ward's good graces was actually an impressive testimony to his acknowledgement of my superiority. But I am getting carried away here; for, to tell the truth, it was no great matter to be superior to the Yeti.

One Saturday morning, Imelda and I found ourselves alone at the breakfast table. My parents always breakfasted early, and Uncle Affleck was in Edinburgh for a regimental dinner the previous night and not expected back until the afternoon. The dishes on the hot-plate included grilled mushrooms, and, a prey, I admit, to a certain obsession, I began to dilate on Restorick's knowledge of the toxic effects of certain rare species of fungus to be found in boggy places on our estate. Imelda shuddered instinctively at the name of the tinker, yet she seemed oddly fascinated by what I had to say, staring at me intently with her great, wide, soft grey eyes. She offered nothing very much in reply but when we had finished eating she said suddenly, with an abruptness that seemed to come from a rapid, difficult resolution,

'Would you come with me, Frank, I'd like to show you something.'

I was thoroughly taken aback by the change in her attitude, and followed her wordlessly as she led the way upstairs to her bedroom. Strange to say, I had never been there, for she lived up a little side-stair near the quarters of Uncle Affleck, who guarded her virtue like some Cerberus, and I had never dared to pass his rooms in order to visit my dear friend. Judge of my astonishment when, having opened the door, she took my hand to lead me over the threshold. The room was characterised by an almost nun-like asceticism. There were no ornaments, and only a few feminine articles on the dressing table. On the bedside table were photographs of Imelda's parents; on the mantelpiece pride of place was given to a picture of Uncle Affleck as an undergraduate at Lincoln College, Oxford and beside it stood a little phial containing a few drops of a cloudy but colourless liquid.

Imelda sat down on the bed—unmade and still rubber-sheeted, a precaution which I am glad to say now only rarely proved necessary—and patted it to indicate that I should join her, which I was nothing loath to do. She was wearing a big woolly sweater and rather loose blue jeans, but her floppy attire served only to accentuate the fragility and vulnerability of her person. I was greatly aroused.

'You were speaking of poisons,' she began. Then she turned to me with shining eyes, as if about to make some wonderful declaration, but abruptly stood up again, walked to the mantelpiece and indicated the little phial.

'That,' she said, 'is the venom of the snake that killed my father. After it had struck at him it was caught and killed and its venom removed; after his death the venom was given to my mother so that she might always have before her eyes this emblem of man's triumph over the serpent. It is my most treasured possession.'

She spoke with great formality, and as may be imagined I was a little confused by this extraordinary statement. 'I see,' I offered somewhat weakly.

Imelda continued to speak with a kind of inspired, vatic conviction, her slender frame shaken as if by a powerful emotion long suppressed and now at last given its head.

'Frank,' she said, 'we too must triumph over the serpent. We mean a lot to each other—why try to conceal it any longer? We have never spoken of it, of course, but we both know. But there can never be anything between us, you do realise that, don't you? Anything more than friendship, I mean, of course. We will always, I hope, be friends. But you know—you must know—that I am destined to be Hubert's. Nothing can change that!'

I leapt up from the bed and impulsively grabbed Imelda by the hands.

'Imelda! What are you saying? My love, my love! You cannot mean that you are willingly going to give yourself to that monster?'

Imelda frowned angrily and withdrew her hands from mine.

'Don't speak of your brother like that!' she cried peremptorily. 'I won't have it. Hubert is a dear, kind soul. I could never ever hurt him. He has been encouraged for years to assume that one day we will be married. It would break his heart, utterly destroy him, if I were to turn away from him now!'

'But Imelda—you don't love him! You've as good as admitted it! You love me—me! Me alone! You cannot go against nature, you cannot spit in the face of love!'

'That I will never do,' rejoined Imelda passionately, 'but I can, and will, deny myself! Dearest, you must understand it is Uncle Affleck's will,' she went on more gently, taking my hand again. 'You do understand, don't you? I owe everything to Uncle Affleck, everything. He took me in when I was a helpless orphan, rescued me, raised me, became father and mother to me. He is utterly devoted to me—and to the interests of the Agnew family. Hubert will one day be the head of that family; but it is not only that. Hubert has always had a very special place in Uncle's heart. He believes, passionately, that Hubert and I are meant for each other—he has set his heart on our match. I cannot go against him, I just cannot!'

She burst into tears, and threw her head onto my breast. I cradled her in my arms.

'Hush, hush!' I whispered. 'Your tender feelings do you credit, my dearest love. I do understand what you are saying. But the passion between man and woman—the true oneness of soul that exists between you and me—cannot so easily be denied and pushed aside! It is a fact, a colossal force of nature, a giant boulder of reality that stands in your path! Seek to avoid it, to make a track around it, and it will roll on you from behind and crush you utterly!'

Imelda struggled free from me once more and wiped her eyes, which were again full of resolution.

'This won't do,' she said firmly. 'I've said it before and I'll say it again—we must triumph over the serpent—the serpent of temptation, the serpent of coming evil. Be brave, Frank, be strong! I'm being brave and strong; can't you see that?' She smiled bravely and strongly through her tears. I suddenly wanted to go. This was all too much to take in at one sitting–I had to get away and be by myself and absorb it all. I made for the door, feigning hopeless, resigned despair. As I was on my way out she called me back, just as I knew she would.

'Frank,' she cried anxiously, 'one more thing! Please, please keep away from Johnny Restorick. The man is evil: I have reason to know that. Please keep right away from him. I love you.'

I turned away like one possessed, tore out of the house and began striding towards the woods. My mind was in utter turmoil and the adrenalin was coursing through my veins, banishing all peace of mind. Nothing would ever be the same again. I realised, of course, that when Imelda spoke of 'triumph over the serpent' she meant exactly the opposite of what she said. I had no previous experience of women, but reason combined with instinct to tell me that. Had she really wanted to maintain the *status quo*, all she would have to do was nothing. I was still young and irresolute, and for all my grandiose plans to oust Hubert, had made no overt move to declare myself. Indeed, I had been thoroughly demoral-ised by Imelda's policy of distance and avoidance. Yet now she called me up to her bedroom, no less, expressly to inform me that something we had never spoken of must never be! And then rounded off the interview by saying that she loved me!

Everything was in the melting-pot now, all the cards were on the table. My whole being raged with a devouring fever–I longed to be alone among my fungi, my restful, undemanding, endlessly soothing fungi. Rounding a corner into a clearing I came face to face with Johnny Restorick. He greeted me with his usual crooked, half-contemptuous grin. Behind him waddled old Wing Commander, the family bulldog, really regarded by everyone as Hubert's pet.

'The ault yin's gettin' gey past it,' observed Restorick, indicat-ing old Wing Commander with a jerk of his thumb. 'Canna keep up nae longer. Trouble wi's innards an aa. It'd be a kindness tae feenish it fur him.' He nodded to himself, knowingly. 'I could dae it easy.'

'If it could be done humanely . . .' I ventured, a trifle uneasily. I knew that some of the concoctions the tinker had at his disposal could be the reverse of humane.

'Oh, ay,' says he, scratching his head with his hook, 'I could fix that nae bother. See when the vet comes tae a dug with the needle, it kens fine whit's adae. Kens it's fur the chop, like. But a wee bit somethin' in his Pal, like, he'd juist slip away quick. Faur kinder.'

'Well . . . you'd better take it up with Hubert when he gets home,' I replied.

'Oh, ay, Hubert.' He snickered and looked away, narrowing his eyes. 'I'll tak it up wi' Hubert right enough.' He nodded secretively to himself and went on his way.

It must have been about this time that the most damning rumours about Restorick began circulating locally. He had always had the reputation of an unscrupulous womaniser, and was said to have more than one bastard in the neighbourhood; but on this occasion, it seemed, he had treated a local girl in a way which went far beyond the bounds of mere irresponsibility and came close to criminal behaviour. The details were withheld from me, but they were such as to oblige even my placid and dithering sire to make an unaccustomed moral stand, or at least a token protest. At any rate, I heard him making representations in quite forceful terms to Uncle Affleck that Restorick should be told to go. Uncle Affleck rejected the suggestion out of hand. The rumours were unfounded calumnies, he claimed, instigated by a restive tenant who harboured a grudge against himself. He could personally vouch for Restorick's character and integrity. Johnny had lost his hand during the war in saving Uncle Affleck's life, and he would stand by him now and whenever it might be necessary. Having made this clear, Sir Robert walked out of the room and there was no further argument; but for several days after that he went around ostentatiously whistling the old air, 'No one will part me from my Johnny'.

I, however, had more pressing matters on my mind than the peccadilloes of Restorick. My relations with Imelda began to take on a see-saw pattern, the ups and downs being more or less strictly identifiable with the university terms and vacations respectively. Even when Hubert was absent, it is true, our intimacies were brief and circumscribed, and Imelda showed no real sign of going back on her resolution to 'triumph over the serpent'. She still avoided going for walks with me, for instance (no doubt for fear of meeting Uncle Affleck), or remaining in my company when no one else was around. But long, meaning looks were often exchanged, hands were held under tables, knees touched, occasionally there was a fleeting, stolen kiss. When my relatively unobservant parents were in the vicinity she enjoyed flirting with danger in this provocative manner, but she never dared attempt it if there were the slightest possibility that Uncle Affleck might appear. Looking back upon it, I am amazed that I contented myself for so long with such crumbs dropped, as it were, from the Yeti's table.

With that doughty metaphysician's every reappearance, the whole atmosphere would change utterly. I would now be addressed frequently, openly and with complete cousinly natural-ness by the shameless young lady. I would be dragged off for walks through the woods with the supposedly amorous pair, involved in all their doings, just so that Hubert, Uncle Affleck and all the world could see how utterly innocent and cousinly were our relations. I had to endure watching her hold Hubert's pudgy hand, give him little pecks on the cheek, call him 'darling', pretend to be coy with him. I almost began to feel sorry for the poor oaf, who was of course wholly unaware that he was being patronised. This affectation of treating me like a dear friend, one who was so dear that it was unthinkable that anything so special-ised and limiting as sexual interest could enter one's relations with him, I found far more demeaning than the coldness of avoidance which had preceded our mutual declarations. And the most awful thing about it was that it was *not* just a show for the benefit of Hubert, Uncle Affleck and the rest: it was also intended as a serious message to me, and most of all, of course, to herself. It was as if she were saying, 'This—this that I am sharing with Hubert—this is real, this is what is, this is what is to be. The rest—those declarations, those passions, those tears, those stolen kisses—that was all a madness, a madness of no significance. Even if it were to happen again—and it might—it still would be only that. It is not

real. This is real–isn't it? Yes, of course, we can all see that it is.
I can even see that it is myself.'

Let me give an example. During his first year at St. Andrews,
Hubert's pestilential digestive system had gone from bad to
worse. He belched and farted uncontrollably, and our meal times
at Lemington were a minor foretaste of purgatory when the
northern Leibnitz was at home. About the Christmas season of his
second year he was diagnosed as suffering from a duodenal ulcer,
and went on a bland diet and a strict regime of alkalines. At this
time Imelda showed a quite exaggerated concern for his welfare
and petted him like a poor innocent baby, when everyone knew
quite well that his ailment was the result of nothing other than an
undisciplined appetite. But her attentions were all part of the
cultivation of that atmosphere of a kind of playful domesticity
which had to be carried to unseemly extremes just so that she
herself might be fully persuaded that it was not an act.

For all the wilfulness that went into these efforts, however,
there were times when Imelda dropped her guard and was
unable to conceal her delight in the marriage of minds which
existed between us, and when her sheer physical excitement
at my presence animated her into careless and uncontrollable
enthusiasm. On such occasions, I observed, Hubert, with a kind
of animal sensitivity that could not possibly have been conscious,
instinctively dropped back into the position of the third, the
excluded one, that was officially mine. One such occasion
occurred one beautiful June evening towards the beginning of his
second long vacation. Imelda had heard a rumour of a nightingale
which could sometimes be heard in the woods near the river about
the twilight hour; and though I had always been told that nightin-
gales could nowadays be found only south of the Trent, while we
were north of the Tweed, I thought it pleasant to humour rather
than to disillusion her. She was bubbling over with excitement, a
kind of enchantment was over her, and this nightingale, after all,
had to do with nothing but our love. So the three of us strolled
down the thickly wooded path, heading for the gorge; Imelda and
I walked side by side, a little apart, and the Yeti trailed behind us,
grunting and snuffling vilely. The magic of early summer was on

the woods, the trees were full of birdsong, an air of tense yet beneficent expectancy was all about us.

At length we arrived at the foot of the tree which the nightingale was said to favour; Imelda put her finger to her lips and glanced up at me with eyes almost bursting with happiness and expectation. Then, as we listened, scarcely daring to breathe, Hubert suddenly rent the evening stillness apart with a shattering and toxic fart. No nightingale could conceivably have survived it. Even old Wing Commander, who had been waddling in our wake, shot off into the undergrowth; as we stood in numbed silence the cracking of twigs and swishing of bracken continued to speak distantly of his panic-stricken flight. Imelda tried at first to pretend that nothing had happened, but it was clearly and palpably impossible–the little idyll had been destroyed for ever. She sighed low and gently, but long, long, and in the dying light a tear could be seen glistening in her brimming eye. Three days later, their engagement was announced.

III

The betrothal of Hubert and Imelda brought with it a subtle alteration in the balance of power. It is perhaps not so surprising as one might at first suppose that this change was in my favour. The formal declaration constituted by an engagement acted as a kind of restraining frame, within which what Imelda regarded as the madness of our love might bloom and riot and disport itself, securely contained by an encirclement of iron circumstance beyond which it would not be permitted to grow. That, at any rate, was the theory, or at least the unformulated feeling. Then again, Imelda was probably sensitive to the danger that, faced with this formidable setback, I might cut my losses and surrender the field to the Yeti. That she assuredly did not want, and given my enthralled condition there was never any likelihood of its happening. But in all this Imelda's emotions were doubtless contradictory and confused. Whatever the proximate causes of her commitment to Hubert might be–pity, longing for safety, sense of duty, gratitude and obedience towards Uncle Affleck–its ultimate causation must lie in some quarrel she was conducting with herself. Was she, perhaps, punishing herself for the death of her parents? I spent a lot of time in the next few months pondering such questions, for if I could discover the answers, then I would know how to act, and on that would depend the future happiness of both of us. In this state of mind I found it hard to concentrate my faculties on *The Fungi of Berwickshire*; but my supposed labours on this *magnum opus* gave me an excuse for mooching about the estate on my own, to the obvious irritation and embitterment of Uncle Affleck, who was by this time undoubtedly aware of my thwarted aspirations towards his ward.

One morning, mooning about in a dwalm with all this on my mind, I wandered into the gloomy, dark stables where I had so often sought peace and solace as a child. It must have been about six months after the engagement; I certainly remember that it was midwinter. I turned a corner–the very corner, in fact, round which I had first encountered Johnny Restorick–and was confronted by a truly appalling sight. Old Wing Commander lay dead before me. He lay half propped up on his back and hunkers against an old sack of manure: his staring eye was dimmed by an opaque film, his mouth open in a snarling grimace of fear and loathing, a dreadful parody of the welcoming smile which had so often animated his wrinkled old visage in life, his upper lip pulled up and caught on one of his horizontally protruding teeth. A stake had been driven through his heart.

I knew at once, somehow, that this was the work of Restorick. It was not merely the association with the spot where this horror lay; in some inexpressible way this bore Restorick's spiritual stamp. The stake, of course, had been inserted after death. It is no easy matter to drive a stake through the heart of a live bulldog, even an old and ailing one, especially when handicapped by having a hook instead of a hand. But I did not doubt that Johnny had carried out his undertaking to do away with the old fellow. In the year that had passed since our brief conversation on the subject, old Wing Commander's 'trouble wi's innards' had certainly worsened alarmingly, and, if one may be permitted the

expression, offensively. It would indeed have been a kindness to
have put him out of his misery. But looking at the expression
which had frozen on his face at death, I doubted all too sadly the
humanity of the method. As to the stake, it must have been
intended by Restorick to make some symbolic statement. Indeed,
I had the uneasy feeling that it was meant to communicate some
evil message to myself.

I was so shocked by my discovery that I could not find it in me
to speak of it to anyone. I had been very fond of the old dog, and
Imelda had doted on him. Hubert, his true master, was far from
home. So far as I am aware, no one but myself saw the uncovered
body. Later the same day, Uncle Affleck gave out that, finding the
old soul moaning in agony, he had administered powerful pain-
killers before sending to Duns for the vet to have him put to sleep.
Once more, he appeared to be shielding Restorick. Early the
following morning he stage-managed a bizarre and, to my mind,
offensive funeral rite. A shallow trench had been dug by the ha-ha,
and the body was carried, wrapped in an old travelling-rug, from
the stables to the grave by an impassive Restorick, who bore it on
his outstretched forearms with his one hand and his hook protruding beyond the folds. Before the corpse was deposited in the
grave, Uncle Affleck delivered a tasteless and facetious, but merci-
fully short, effusion, and as the earth was shovelled over the body
he gave a military salute. As he did so, I experienced a keen
surprise that it was not a *Nazi* salute; and at that moment I realised
of whom it was that Uncle Affleck had always subliminally
reminded me: it was Sir Oswald Mosley.

This perception caused my taut nerves to snap, and I fell into
a fit of hysterical laughter and had to rush away from the close of
the funeral proceedings. I ran into the morning room where I
knew Imelda would be waiting, for she had told me earlier that
she could not bear to watch as old Wing Commander, the silent
companion of so many of our woodland wanderings, disappeared
for ever beneath the sod. As I fell into her tenderly outstretched
arms I gave way to the heavy, nameless sorrow that was welling
up in my soul, and bursting into convulsive sobs I buried my face
on her shoulder.

'Ah, how you feel, how you feel, dear Superbo!' crooned

Imelda. 'Sometimes I have thought you harsh and cruel, but now I see how tender-hearted you really are. My dear love, it is a heavy fate which keeps us apart ...'; and so on and so forth. We rehearsed the old arguments for and against her nuptials with the Yeti, and as usual got no further forward. Indeed, this situation remained materially unaltered during Hubert's entire four years at St Andrews. Somehow or other he had scraped into the honours class, and there was even talk of his doing a year of postgraduate work before the marriage took place. This at least gave me time.

The next incident of importance in this long drawn-out saga occurred on the Christmas Day of Hubert's last year as an undergraduate. A year had passed since the death of old Wing Commander. Imelda and I had been behaving with considerable circumspection, and I believe that even Uncle Affleck's morbid suspicions had been to some degree allayed. He seemed, at any rate, cheerlessly resigned to the fact that *The Fungi of Berwickshire* was to constitute my life's work, and had more or less ceased to agitate that I should be obliged to depart from Lemington and take up some form of 'gainful employment'. Since old Wing Commander's horrible end I had been extremely cautious in my dealings with Restorick, though I had not entirely broken off relations with him. We had never spoken directly of the incident, but Restorick had occasionally dropped hints that I was in some way implicated in the old bulldog's death, or at least compromised by it. Hubert had been inconsolable when he was told the news, and, it seemed in reaction, suffered renewed and repeated attacks of internal commotion.

After Christmas Dinner on the day in question, the ladies had retired to the drawing room, while Uncle Affleck, my father and myself remained behind to enjoy a glass of port and a cigar. Hubert had already been obliged to retire to bed, stuffed with turkey and plum pudding and belching uncontrollably. The atmosphere among us three remaining men was dreary and depressing. My father and Uncle Affleck, though not on unfriendly terms, never had anything to say to one another, and Uncle Affleck made a point of disagreeing tetchily with everything that I contributed in the way of social discourse. Eventually I wearied of his carping ill-will and left the room, drifting out onto the terrace to finish my cigar. The night was clear and keen without being unpleasantly cold, the stars were flickering brightly and a quarter moon hung over the woods beyond the clock-tower of the stable block. I had been leaning on the parapet for about five minutes, drinking in the beauty of the evening and lost in contemplation, when I heard a slight sound behind me and turned to find Imelda standing before me, her face upraised in tense, joyful expectation.

She was wrapped in a white angora shawl, and sheathed in a stunning green silk dress; around her neck was the gold necklace with a single ruby which she had been wearing on the day of her arrival at Lemington. I took a step towards her and we remained for a moment gazing at one another in a kind of wrapt mutual adoration. A romantic picture we must have made as we stood there, I strikingly handsome in the moonlight, a paper hat perched at a jaunty angle on my noble brow, she with her ghostly-pale, elfin visage upturned towards mine. A moment more, and her seeking mouth came up to meet the proud curve of my lips. Wine, and the season, and the magic of the night, and the imperious call of young love which may not be denied, banished all caution as we closed in an embrace free from the least hesitancy or restraint.

A stentorian roar from the direction of the French windows brought our ecstasy to a premature close. Disengaging and whirling round, we beheld Uncle Affleck advancing upon us with great strides, his face the colour of a turkey-cock's, his eyes bulging with fury and the veins standing out on his temples. Pushing Imelda roughly aside, he administered a great cuff to my shoulder with the heel of his palm, which sent me staggering against the parapet, and before I had a chance to recover myself, slapped me resoundingly across the side of the face, making my ears sing. Two factors alone restrained me from felling him with a single blow: firstly his age, and secondly, and more important, my concern for Imelda, who could scarcely have borne such a set-to between her lover and her adored guardian. With a colossal effort of self-control, clenching my fists convulsively in order to curb my surging emotions, I stared at him my mute defiance.

'Contemptible wretch!' he bellowed. 'You would play the Lothario, would you? You would betray your absent brother,

sully your cousin's virtue? I will alter the angle of that fine nose
of yours, so help me Jupiter ...'

Imelda rushed between us and grabbed Uncle Affleck by the
arm.

'Uncle, uncle!' she cried heart-rendingly, 'Frank is not to blame!
The fault is mine, mine alone! It means nothing, I swear to you!
It was just the wine we've drunk, the spirit of Christmas, the
beauty of the evening ... don't hurt poor Frank, I beg you!
Punish me, if you like, punish me, but don't touch poor Frank!'

Uncle Affleck seemed prepared to take her at her word, for after
a moment's hesitation, dismissing me with a snort of contempt, he
swivelled round on his heel, and taking Imelda harshly by the arm
dragged her indoors. She threw me back a despairing, beseeching
look, her face deathly pale, and then disappeared behind the
French windows with her brutal keeper.

This was a serious event. The following morning a deputation
consisting of Uncle Affleck and my father came to visit me in my
bedroom, where I was sketching fungi. I was cautioned, almost as
if they had been policemen and I a criminal suspect—Uncle Affleck
a fierce and formidable sergeant, my father a shy and inexperi-
enced constable. I was ordered, on pain of instant expulsion from
Lemington, to keep away from Imelda, and to say nothing
whatever about what had occurred to anyone, and least of all to
Hubert. Hubert was to be shielded at all costs from the slightest
inkling of his fiancée's possible disaffection. A family conference
would be held in two or three weeks' time, after his return to St
Andrews, when my fate and that of Imelda would be decided;
until then I was to regard myself as on probation.

Sir Robert was, of course, the mouthpiece of authority; my
father stood to his left and a little behind him all the time he was
speaking, with his hands twisting nervously behind his back, his
clerical collar hanging away from his scrawny neck, his white hair
in wispy disarray, smiling inanely and nodding as his brother-in-
law laid down the law. All this time I continued calmly to sketch
a section of a rare puff-ball, and kept my own counsel, saying
nothing and maintaining a discreet, bland, neutral kind of expression, to Uncle Affleck's intense irritation. When he had finished
speaking he remained standing there, awaiting a response; since

he had not asked me any question, however, I found myself under no obligation to comment.

'Do you agree to our proposal, sir, yes or no?' he snapped at last.

'I agree to your *proposal*,' I replied. I emphasised the noun in such a way as to imply that if their message had been put to me in any form *other* than that of a proposal, they could have stuffed it up their asses.

For a week after that Imelda was confined to her room with a case of diplomatic influenza; after her recovery I saw her only at meal times. She kept her eyes lowered modestly in my presence, and was shyly attentive to the needs of the metaphysical Yeti. A couple of days after that great philosopher's departure the family conference took place in the library on a dull and gloomy Saturday morning. My parents and Imelda were already present when I arrived, Imelda pale but demure, my mother stiff and unbending, my father looking as if he would have preferred to be on the planet Tralfamadore. Then Uncle Affleck strode in wearing a carnation and carrying a clipboard. To my utter astonishment, Restorick followed him in, closed the door behind him and remained standing beside it, staring impassively through the window into the middle distance and picking his nose. I made at once to protest, but Imelda silenced me with a shake of the head and a warning look at once commanding and terror-stricken. I shrugged my shoulders in resigned disbelief. Uncle Affleck opened the proceedings by announcing, in a gentle and benevolent, but at the same time a *directive* tone of voice, that he believed that Imelda had something which she wished to say. Imelda cleared her throat, picked up a little tortoiseshell ash-tray on the coffee table in front of her, and turning it around ceaselessly in her hands, delivered herself of the amazing effusion which follows.

'My dear family,' she began, 'to whom I owe so much, I have repaid you ill for your measureless kindness to a poor orphan. I have betrayed your trust, and in a moment of thoughtlessness have merited the loss of my dear Hubert. I thank God that he has no knowledge of what occurred, which will never occur again. I beg your forgiveness. Blame–not me, not even poor Frank–but the serpent who has seduced us both. We were weak, not wicked.

I have no improper feelings for Frank, and if he has any esteem for me he will dismiss as utterly unworthy any such feelings that *he* may harbour. If I am not considered now to have renounced my hope to be my beloved Hubert's wife, I shall be his *faithful* wife for ever. If that is not to be, I shall live and die a virgin.'

I listened with my mouth open, uncertain as to whether I was hallucinating, or whether perhaps I had wandered by mistake into some Stalinist show-trial of the thirties. Such was the unreality of what I had heard, that I felt not even a flutter of resentment at Imelda's denial of myself. Uncle Affleck turned to me with a smile of triumph, as if he had just delivered some devastating pre-emptive strike.

'You now know, young man,' he said, 'your position in regard to Imelda. In regard to your future, two possibilities lie open to you. You can leave here tomorrow to make your own way in the world; if you choose to remain you will start work on Monday as a labourer on the estate. For the next few months you are likely to be employed on logging duties. Your father wishes you to know that he will tolerate no longer your remaining here in a condition of parasitism. State your choice.'

I had no choice. 'I remain,' I replied, without stating specifically that I accepted the condition; and rewarded my father with a look of withering contempt. He stirred uneasily, and a sort of change came over his complexion such as might have answered for a blush in one whose circulation ran on carrot juice rather than blood. My future settled, Uncle Affleck removed a shiny brochure from his clipboard, and began reading aloud, in an equivocal tone of voice that might equally have been taken to be admiring or satirical, of the merits and advantages of a finishing school for young ladies at Montreux. As he came to particularly choice phrases, he would pause for a moment and peer over the top of his glasses at Imelda with a quizzical, theatrical expression: he was wonderfully delighted with himself. Imelda's lips quivered and she looked as if at any moment she might burst into floods of tears; and when he finished reading and turned to her with the words, 'Well, dear Imelda, what do you say to that?', the flood-gates were opened.

A harrowing scene followed. Imelda sobbed that it would be an unbearable torture to her to be away from Lemington, from my parents, from Uncle Affleck–above all to be so far from her cherished Hubert. Yes, she actually said that, and with great appearance of sincerity; the only person, apparently, for whom she would not be pining in her sorrowful exile on the banks of Lake Geneva was myself. My mother took up the cudgels on behalf of the finishing school: it would broaden Imelda's outlook, improve her languages, enlarge her restricted circle of acquaintance, give her the social confidence and *savoir faire* of which a narrow existence on a remote Berwickshire estate had unavoidably deprived her. Hubert was undoubtedly soon to embark on a professional academic career of the highest distinction, and Imelda, as his wife, would require to be in command of wide conversation and varied social skills and to exhibit a mature capacity to mix with all classes and conditions of men and women. My father took no part in the conversation, but occasionally nodded benignly, with an expression on his face such as he might have assumed had he been attempting to give the impression that he was taking an intelligent interest in a conversation being conducted in Serbo-Croat.

Uncle Affleck, while listening to these pleas and counterarguments, wore a judicial expression, sitting with his leatherpatched elbows on the library table and his finger-tips pressed lightly together, occasionally parting them and bringing them together again as an aid, one was to assume, to achieving clarity of judgement. When the females had eventually lapsed into weary silence, he began by stating that as a matter of general principle he was in entire agreement with everything his sister had said. He paused for a moment in order to allow us to savour fully the coming of the 'but'.

'There is, however, a practical matter to be taken into consideration. It is a matter of some delicacy, but I am afraid that I cannot avoid bringing it into play. It is this: Imelda's little weakness is not yet *entirely* overcome ... Largely, largely overcome,' he added expansively, as if in deference to Imelda's obviously acute confusion, 'but not yet entirely. There has even, I believe, been a slight relapse in the past couple of weeks–am I right, mother?'

'You are indeed,' my mother could not forebear to acknowledge.

Restorick, hitherto expressionless, was now smirking vilely.

'Am I right, Imelda?' Uncle Affleck pursued with wicked
gentleness. Imelda nodded mutely.

'Yes ... yes,' said Sir Robert in the same gentle tone. 'And in
that circumstance it would, I think, be needlessly cruel to plunge
poor Imelda into the maelstrom of communal living. Perhaps,
anyway, they wouldn't have her,' he added with the ghost of an
icy smile.

The cunning old man had come to Imelda's rescue at the
expense of humiliating her utterly; it was perfectly clear that he
had never had the least intention of having her sent to the
finishing school at Montreux. This option having been formally
rejected, to Imelda's obvious relief in spite of the sadism to which
she had just been subjected, consideration was given to an alterna-
tive. Uncle Affleck, vociferously supported by his sister, made a
number of leading remarks to the effect that the devil made work
for idle hands. Glances of barbed contempt directed at myself
made it clear what kind of devil's work he had in mind. The
upshot was that, in order to forestall such a calamity, Imelda was
to be put to work in the kitchen for an initial period of six months.
Our sentences having been thus passed and ratified by the 'family
conference', the meeting was ended to the obviously intense
satisfaction of Uncle Affleck and the insolently presumptuous
Restorick.

The whole affair had been stage-managed by Uncle Affleck even
more outrageously than the funeral of old Wing Commander,
whether or not with Imelda's collusion, willing or coerced. Her
part in it was shadowy and uncertain, though it was clear enough
that she was far from being privy to every nuance of her
guardian's tactics. As to my mother, she was a mere pawn, being
far too stupid to be granted anything but a contingent and passive
role in such a subtle game. Strange to say, the performance
increased my grudging admiration for Sir Robert's mastery of
affairs. All was planned with military precision and executed with
great psychological finesse as well as decisiveness and resolve. It

was impossible to withhold from such a tactician a measure of qualified respect.

And so it transpired that, for the better part of half a year, two fine-grained and richly endowed young people from an ancient Border family were reduced to the status of lumberjack and kitchenmaid respectively. I was far more angry and resentful on behalf of Imelda than for myself, for my provisional and temporary acceptance of the situation in which I found myself was finally my own choice, in essence a tactical move: I was biding my time and recruiting my forces, awaiting my opportunity. I knew that Uncle Affleck had assigned me to work which he was convinced would be too hard for me, which I would soon do anything to escape, even to leaving Lemington and Imelda. That was the end he had been aiming for all along, and I was absolutely determined to thwart and disappoint him. Scholar and aesthete I might be, but I was also hard as nails, spare and lithe, without an ounce of excess flesh on my body. It took me a little time to accustom myself to the rhythms of manual labour, and to grow callouses on my hands, but when I had done so, few of the other young fellows hired for the logging could hold a candle to me in respect of strength, hardihood, stamina and sheer capacity for hard work. Above all, I never let a word of complaint pass my lips, however unremitting the labour or exacting the demands of the foreman. Within a month or two, not only had I forced Uncle Affleck to accord me proper respect, he obviously found it hard to deny himself expression of his reluctant admiration.

Poor Imelda's case was very different. She had been given no real choice, and was utterly in the power of Uncle Affleck. Her fate was inseparable from Lemington, and she had to be bound by its laws. Besides, she was utterly unprepared for any life beyond its bounds. Psychologically fragile and physically delicate, she was now, totally unaccustomed to physical labour, consigned to hours of drudgery day after day at the kitchen sink, under the ill-disposed eye of that unlikeable harridan, Mrs Brumfitt the cook. Imelda and I had been formally forbidden to meet except in the presence of a third party, and our respective duties now kept us apart even during most meal times; but when I did see Imelda she looked ever paler, sadder and more exhausted. It was only when she began to exhibit symptoms of ill-health so definite and worrying as to threaten her marriage to Hubert, that the cruel regimen was ultimately abandoned. By that time it was in any case about to end for both of us, thanks to the final and triumphant return of the afore-mentioned doughty metaphysician from St Andrews.

IV

Incredible to relate, the Bigfoot had graduated with first class honours in Philosophy. How this could possibly have occurred I can in no way explain; it is one of those mysteries before which one can only bow in silent wonder. No doubt he had worked ponderously hard; certainly he had remained in the little old grey city over the Easter vacation, poring over his tomes while I sawed and heaved logs and Imelda scrubbed pots and pans. He remained, need one say, as dim-witted as ever; but he had been admitted to Lincoln College, Oxford—Uncle Affleck's old college, naturally—to do a year's postgraduate work before seeking a university appointment. His marriage to Imelda had therefore been postponed until the following summer.

Imelda was allowed to accompany my parents to the graduation. Uncle Affleck chose to forego the pleasure of watching his adored protégé being capped, ostensibly because of restrictions on ticket allocation, but perhaps in reality so that he could keep an eye on myself and ensure that my nose was kept to the grindstone until the last possible moment. Imelda and I were to be released from our labours so that Hubert might be spared any knowledge of the untoward events which had led to our sentences. The graduation party stayed at Rusack's Hotel for several nights: it was almost Imelda's first trip away from Lemington since her arrival there nearly twelve years before. In her exhausted state of health the excitement attendant upon her dear Hubert's triumph, together with sudden exposure to the great wide world, was almost too much for her, and I understand that at the celebration dinner she became disgracefully intoxicated.

The Yeti returned to Lemington beaming with self-complacency and good will. I can see him now, in his white, lightweight jacket, striped shirt and red and blue spotted bow-tie, leaning on the parapet of the terrace puffing away at his pipe, gazing with a benign twinkle in his eye towards the distant Cheviot, and thinking thoughts of positively Platonic ideality, while Imelda hung adoringly on his arm. It always struck me as ironical that Hubert, whose wits remained in reality so earth-bound, believed himself soaring in ethereal space, while I, modestly bent towards the humble fungus, could effortlessly leap in the spirit to heights from which our home-grown philosopher was for ever excluded. Be that as it may, for several weeks that summer Imelda appeared positively to dote on her endearingly self-approving intended.

The three of us were constantly together during that long and glorious summer. It seemed, indeed, to be part of Hubert's mood of complacent self-confidence to draw me into the circle of their warmth: all cause of rivalry, he felt, was now past, and it became him to be gracious and magnanimous in victory. So sweetly did Imelda cleave to him that even Uncle Affleck, I believe, dropped his guard a little and almost ceased to regard me as a serious threat to his plans. No doubt he was congratulating himself on his acumen and on the apparently unqualified success of his strategy: and who could blame him? Certainly not I.

But as the weeks passed, the unnaturally bright picture began gradually and subtly to alter. More delicate emotional tints began to emerge, intimations of shadow started to flit over the stolid features of the Yeti. Imelda clung to his arm still, but less spontaneously, even in the end a little desperately. I made a point of never allowing them to be alone together if I could find a way of preventing it; and my constant and no doubt intoxicating proximity before long began to have the desired effect on Imelda. Increasingly often, she would let go of Hubert and place a gentle, cousinly hand on my elbow as she pointed out to me a choice fungal specimen that had flashed into her vision, or paused breathlessly to catch some rare and fleeting snatch of birdsong; and from these little moments, without our conscious intention, Hubert was not blatantly but all the same quite definitely distanced. So there came at last a day when it was once again our *threeness* which accompanied us like an unseen presence, an invisible fourth party; not three people but one soul, not that at all, but the subtle inter-weavings of our inter-relationship, its delicate yet quivering tensions, working away perpetually just below the surface of our common life, becoming gradually more definite, slowly more conscious, ready to assume and assert its own inoppugnable reality.

Hubert began to fall back. He fell back, he lost ground, in Imelda's affections which he had for a time unnaturally dominated; and as he did so he increasingly fell back literally too, trailing behind us on our communal walks, sometimes absenting himself for short periods, as if he actually wanted us to be alone together. A dark, abstracted mood would come upon him, a haunted sadness was in the meditative puffing of his pipe; all self-complacency had fallen away from him. Then he would slip unobtrusively apart, sometimes without comment, sometimes muttering some vague, half-articulated excuse.

Imelda and I both knew what this was about, and each knew that the other knew, but at first Imelda mutely clung to the pretence that she didn't. Or rather, more precisely, we knew *what* it was, but we did not fully know *why* it was. What exactly was it that made Hubert do it? Was it self-abnegation, was it goodness— an inappropriate, misguided goodness, of course, but still goodness; or was it merely weakness? Or was it perhaps, something altogether darker, something which it would be better for the peace of mind of all three of us not to look at too closely? Had he, for instance, come to want so much that Imelda and myself should feel guilty, should take to heart the pain which we were inflicting upon him, that in order that we should have occasion more acutely to do so, he undertook to provide us with the occasion?

One beautiful day in early September, Hubert seemed suddenly revivified. A warm, expansive mood was on him, and a sunny enthusiasm animated his expression as he proposed that the three of us should take a drive a few miles up the road in the little MG sports car which my parents had given him as a graduation present, and then climb up to the prehistoric fortification known as Edin's Hall Broch, and perhaps afterwards up Cockburn Law, which overlooks it and which commands fine and extensive views over almost the whole of Berwickshire. All three of us had been to the broch on several occasions as children, but now we would see it with a more knowledgeable eye, appreciate its unusual archaeological features and the peculiar qualities of its structure, gain a proper realisation of its strategic significance. Imelda and I were nothing loath; a picnic lunch was prepared, and together with two or three bottles of beer packed in a small rucksack, and we set off on our little expedition at about eleven in the morning.

Our way led first through some pine woods, then across the rocky pools of the Whitadder by a rickety wooden suspension bridge. After walking up-river for a few hundred yards we crossed a meadow and began to climb on a rough track between cultivated fields, negotiating stiles over several drystane dykes. As we climbed, Hubert began to complain of physical distress. The condition of his ulcer was fluctuating: the previous spring, under the strain of his impending final examinations, it had given him severe and constant pain, but with his academic triumph had subsided with dramatic swiftness, and all summer had lain quiescent. Now, however, he complained of sudden nausea and giddiness, though he was showing no obvious visible signs of illness. When after about half an hour we reached the rock-strewn sward immediately below the broch, he subsided on the grass in apparent exhaustion. He seemed oddly abstracted and agitated, absent-mindedly ignored questions and muttered vague speculations about the possible causes of the ulcer's renewed activity.

Imelda unpacked the lunch and Hubert decided that a little something in his stomach might help to settle it; he ate a couple of sandwiches and, perhaps unwisely, drank a bottle of Export. Almost immediately he began to belch with nerve-jangling and offensive loudness, apologising occasionally but making no attempt to moderate the explosive force of his eructations. Imelda and I looked at him curiously. Undoubtedly he was worried and upset about something, but I could not avoid the impression that he was exaggerating his physical discomfort, nor the suspicion that he was actually manufacturing some at least of those cataclysmic burps. Soon he ceased talking altogether, and ignoring completely the glorious view of the richly wooded Whitadder valley spread beneath us, stared at his feet in gloomy and dispirited dejection, continuing to belch from time to time, but with gradually diminishing vigour. Disturbed and embarrassed by his mood, and wondering what it might portend, Imelda and I alike lapsed into silence.

Eventually, as if he had come suddenly to a difficult but definite resolution, he stood up, and without looking at either of us said that he was going back down and would wait for us by the bridge. He wanted to be alone by the river until his acute bout of discomfort had passed. Imelda took hold of his arm and began to protest that she would go back with him while I examined the broch and climbed the law, but he shook her off almost roughly and began at once to plod heavily downhill with his eyes to the ground.

'Take the car home if you're feeling bad, darling,' called Imelda after him, 'we'll hitch a lift!', but he made no reply. When he had walked a few more paces he raised his hand and waved it once, with a wide, slow sweep, but never turned his head. We stood staring at him as he strode doggedly on down a steep sheep-track, crossed a swampy patch and passed through a little gate and along the edge of a field. He would not turn back. We sighed and faced each other and our eyes were full of unspoken words; Imelda's lips were parted in wonder and expectation and my heart thumped painfully. I took her hand and we walked in silence towards the broch.

Edin's Hall Broch, said by some to take its name from a mythical giant, the Red Etin of Ireland, is an early Dark Age structure unique in Scotland. Of far wider extent than any of the northern brochs, it encloses in its great, low-walled circle a large open space, but an inner wall forms a number of chambers, whether domestic or defensive in purpose I am ignorant. We stepped into the broch through the narrow entrance, crossed the grassy interior and entered one of these chambers opposite. Nearly two millennia ago, perhaps, had some man and some woman done in this spot what we were about to do? I took Imelda in my arms and kissed her, and a sense of timelessness, of being a fleeting but somehow immortal actor upon history's inexorably moving screen, filled me with a sense of awe, of my own littleness, even while it inflamed my transitory but uncontainable desire.

Frantically we started throwing our clothes off: the day was wonderfully fine and clear and an autumn sun shone brightly from a sky of flawless blue, but the hint of September chill already in the air added a *frisson* to Imelda's shiver of expectation. I drew her to me and we lay down on the thick rough grass amid the sheep and rabbit droppings; and there rushed back on me from childhood that sense of Imelda's essential wildness and her untamed nature, the powerful primitive force which issued from her fragile frame, a gusting, moaning wind of the spirit which stirred my own spirit to ecstatic yearning ...

Novice that I was, I was guilty of a few unconscionable fumblings, but Imelda was my sure and instinctive guide, and soon our love was finding expression in a passionate, swiftly driving rhythm, so unflagging that it threatened to bring my own contribution to a premature and explosive end. Imelda knew that I could not hold on much longer, and pushed and twisted frantically, giving vent to great striving, gasping groans and thumping her pubic bone against mine in a mad race against time! I hung on bravely, holding my forces poised in an ecstasy of suspension, until I saw her eyes widen and deepen into great bottomless pools, and heard her call swing towards mystical triumph, and as she climaxed I released my contained fire with volcanic force ... I feared that Hubert, down in the dell, would hear her piercing cry of fulfilment. What a performance from two such neophytes in love!

Thus was a love consummated that had been twelve years in growing. What could we say? We said little, but lay long entwined within our prehistoric love-nest, gazing up at the huge blue sweep of the firmament, broken only rarely by a bird passing overhead, a gentle breeze playing upon our bare flesh. We made love again, and this time it was slow and rich and powerful and seemed to pass into our bodies from the very earth itself on which we lay. The afternoon wore on, and still we lay there. We had set out to climb Cockburn Law, and instead we had scaled Mount Venus. At last we knew that it was time to go.

'What now?' I asked as we descended the steep sheep-track.
'How can we be together? What are we going to do?'

'In three weeks' time Hubert will be off to Oxford. We will be
together then, my darling, all the time, all, all the time, and we'll
think what to do. *No one* is going to be able to keep us apart now.
Oh, Superbo, I'm so happy!'

The only post-coital sadness that afternoon was Hubert's. We
came upon him sitting on a rock gazing abstractedly into the
Whitadder, smoking his pipe, lost in gloomy rumination. He
barely responded when we greeted him and enquired after his
health, and he asked us no questions in return. Beside him, lying
under his tobacco-pouch, was Boethius' *The Consolation of Philosophy.*
We drove back in silence, Imelda in the front passenger seat
leaning away from Hubert with her elbow out of the window.
Something about her posture, and about the attitude of resigned
weariness with which Hubert drove his bright little sports car,
made my heart go out to the poor Yeti for perhaps the first time
in my life. Or perhaps it was merely guilt.

A few days of ecstatic happiness followed. We managed to
come together in love once more, this time in Imelda's bedroom
while Uncle Affleck was in Berwick; but all our fleeting lightsome
meetings were ballasted with the sweet delight of happy conspiracy, in its way just as wonderful a thing as the joyful abandon
of fulfilled passion. Even the little frustrations we encountered
seemed beneficent, for we knew that they were but insignificant
pebbles scattered on the smooth path leading to our future
bliss, which would soon be swept clear of all such insignificant
impediments.

But a week later a wholly unexpected blow descended to wreck
our happiness. It was announced by my mother at breakfast that,
in order that the engaged couple should not have to endure a year
of separation, Imelda would accompany Hubert south and live
during his time at Oxford with old friends of my parents in the
Oxfordshire village of Charlton-on-Otmoor. Was not that a
splendid plan? The careless words fell like a hammer-blow and
were succeeded by a charged, expectant silence. Poor Imelda
turned a deathly pale and made distinctly heavy weather of the
quite impossible task of appearing delighted and grateful; Hubert,

who had recovered his spirits only a little since the expedition to
Edin's Hall Broch, made a slightly better show of it, but scarcely
radiated the expected exuberant joy; and Uncle Affleck, whose
brainwave this assuredly was, smirked into his coffee and kept his
own counsel. My father said, 'Yes, splendid plan, quite splendid,'
and kept repeating it while the betrothed couple were responding;
and I chewed an oatcake impassively and thus let it be understood
that the affair was no concern of mine. I was aware of Uncle
Affleck directing sidelong glances at me to gauge my reaction; it
was clear that his suspicions had been fatally renewed. One could
not but admire his persistence and his resource.

How unstable and ephemeral is human happiness! A little week,
and our brief joy was changed into mourning. We hoped and
trusted, of course, that happiness would return–little did we know
that it was gone for ever, and that for both of us the future, could
we have pierced its veil, would have been seen to stretch before
us in an endless dreary prospect of anguish and misery! Preparations for Imelda's departure began almost immediately after that
fateful breakfast. A few hurried words in private were all that we
could manage. She would be home, fleetingly, for Christmas and
the New Year; in the intervening months we must each of us rack
our brains to devise a *plan*, an infallible scheme for rescuing
Imelda from the Yeti's clutches and restoring her to my arms.
Failure was unthinkable–we could not, must not fail. Fond
mortals! Even as we spoke a fatal seed of disaster was already
growing, a deathly wind blowing which would blast our highest
hopes and wither in the bud the infant flower of love.

V

Do I posture, do I romanticise? Undoubtedly. What else can a
poor madman do, locked away since youth from all the world and
condemned to useless and futile self-analysis, to perpetual self-
condemnation? Why was it that, when Imelda had gone, I began
once again to frequent the society of Restorick, which, since the

shocking outrage of his attendance at the 'family conference', I
had relentlessly shunned? I knew that he was evil: my dear Imelda
had told me so as one who had cause to know, and I had felt it
myself the first instant that my eyes had rested upon him. I knew,
too, that he was the henchman, the confidant and the intimate of
Uncle Affleck, who was the enemy of my happiness, if not indeed
of my person. To consort with such a one was desperately unwise.
Yet, willy-nilly, I was drawn to Restorick. The occasion of our
meetings was always ostensibly to discuss fungi; for with Imelda's
departure I had plunged once more into frenzied work on my
magnum opus and with the autumn fruiting season conditions were
ideal for observation and field-work. But if fungi provided the
occasion, the rapport between us was far more deeply rooted. The
sense of conspiracy, of complicity, of my being subtly *compromised*
by my association with the sinister tinker, which I had felt even
as a child, now returned on me with redoubled force; but there
was an attraction in it too, an exhilarating sense of entering
dangerous waters, of putting to the test my wits and my resourcefulness and my courage.

Our talk that autumn seemed to be all of toxicology: I was
devoting a special chapter of my master-work to this subject. As
I concentrated all my attention on this one aspect of mycology I
was continually astonished by the variety and the ingenuity of the
methods which nature had devised for disturbing or destroying
the human organism. The names of the dangerous or deadly
species had a macabre beauty all of their own, and it was ironical
that many of the most fatal were among the loveliest to behold.
There were the Deadly Inocybe, the Deadly Lepiota and the
Deadly Galerina. There was Fly Agaric, that bright red beauty
with spots of white veil, so common in northern woodlands.
There was the Brown Roll-Rim, with destructive cumulative
effects, and the Death Cap, minute quantities of which caused
death in agony. There was Satan's Bolete with its blushing stalk,
readily confusable with the delicious Spring Bolete. There was
Poison Pie, to be found in magical woodland fairy circles but a
sure recipe for gastric disaster. The Lawyer's Wig was toxic in
conjunction with alcohol, while the Sweating Mushroom contained muscarine, giving rise to sweating, blurred vision and

involuntary muscular tics. The hallucinogenic Liberty Cap, to be found on our lawns and parks, could generate delirium. The cherry-red Sickener induced vomiting, while the Lead Poisoner could kill with cramps, vomiting and diarrhoea. The edible Blusher could be confused with the deadly Panther. But I think my favourite was the Destroying Angel, straight and slender, pure and shining in its whiteness, the hint of a pink tinge on its cap, with a flaring fragile ring and a large volva at the base of the stalk. Fair creature though it be, it is one of the deadliest species of all. Examples of many of these villains could be found in the woods and fields and moorlands of Lemington, and Restorick was familiar with the properties of all of them.

One afternoon in late October I had been looking around for Johnny but could find no trace of him. Lonely and depressed, I fell into my old childhood habit and wandered into the stables to brood in their dark, gloomy and silent recesses. Hearing as I entered a kind of scuffling noise accompanied by stertorous breathing, I halted in astonishment and listened, holding my breath. After the scuffling there came a longish pause, filled only by a sound as of panting, and after about a minute a kind of groan. I was, I must own, terrified. After another protracted pause a voice I thought was Restorick's said, 'And how good he upheld her,' or something like that. After waiting another minute or two I could contain my curiosity no longer, and with a thumping heart stepped forward cautiously and peered round into the corner from which the sounds were coming. It was the very same corner in which, so many years ago, I had first encountered Johnny Restorick, and where I had later made the horrible discovery of old Wing Commander's stake-impaled corpse. The scene I now witnessed, if less horrific, was equally foul and infinitely more degrading.

Huddled in the darksome neuk, Sir Robert Affleck and Johnny Restorick were engaged in an act of gross indecency. The latter was stark naked, but the former was wearing a nightie. Uncle Affleck, facing into the corner (I shall not attempt a description of his posture) remained unaware of my presence, but Restorick, presumably hearing some slight sound I must have made as I advanced, looked over his shoulder, and seeing me, gave me a huge wink and flashed his wry, twisted grin; then continued quite unperturbed with his abominable activity. The expression on his face might appropriately have accompanied the phrase 'All in the day's work'.

It was a particular feature of Restorick's character that he never offered an explanation of anything. The next time I met him I was acutely embarrassed, for I did not see how the event of which I had been an unwilling spectator could possibly pass without comment from one of us. I knew that Johnny would not volunteer anything, but I thought that he might indicate by his mien that he would respond if I were to question him. I could not formulate in any precise way anything I wanted to ask, however: what I really wanted to say was simply 'Why?' or 'Can it be true?' or perhaps 'Often?' But Restorick gave me no opening at all. Though he must have been conscious enough of my consternation, he behaved in every respect as if nothing whatever had happened. He did not even bother to cover my self-conscious silence with talk on some unrelated subject, but simply hummed away under his breath as he often did, until he felt ready to resume the discussion we had embarked upon a few days before on the toxic properties of the Poison Pie.

There was nothing that Restorick might do which would really have surprised me, and after my initial disgust had been digested I found that my feelings about the tinker—never in the least warm, but always somehow involved—had not materially altered. It was not so with Uncle Affleck. In spite of how much our interests and attitudes were at variance, I had always sincerely admired my uncle, and in a peculiar but real way respected him. His single-mindedness, his powers of execution, and his decision seemed to me worthy of tribute. And it was precisely because these qualities were truly present in him, and because they could not honestly be discounted or denied, that I now had to feel ashamed for him. I did not despise or abhor him, I felt rather as I might have done if I were struggling to come to terms with some repressed or denied impulse in my own nature which I felt was vile and resisted even as it demanded entry into consciousness.

Looking back on this incident now, I recall it as a kind of overture to catastrophe. During the next month I sank deeper into

gloom and discouragement: I was no further towards devising a
plan for the rescue of Imelda or the restoration and establishment
of our happiness. Such was still my situation when, during the last
week of November, an extraordinary scurry, fuss and agitation
erupted one morning at Lemington. As usual in relation to any
circumstance touching Imelda, I was not informed of what was
going on, but I was able to pick up enough to gather that a
somewhat distraught telephone call had been received from
Hubert, that the trouble concerned Imelda's health, and that both
of them were expected at Lemington that night. Excitement at the
speedy return of my darling was more than tempered by the
profound misgiving which depressed and paralysed my spirit. It
had been far too dangerous for Imelda to risk writing to me at
Lemington, and I had been left for weeks without any news of
how she was faring at Charlton-on-Otmoor. I was soon to learn.

All day I kept walking up and down near the house; I did not
even dare to go down to the woods or the gorge, lest further news
should arrive during my absence, or the couple appear earlier than
expected. After dark I paced around the downstairs rooms,
nervous and agitated, my heart palpitating, my feet sweating even
in the damp November chill of the inadequately heated mansion
house. At about 6.30 pm, standing alone in the unlighted drawing
room, the curtains still undrawn, I saw the lights of Hubert's MG
beam across the lawn, swing round and slow down in front of the
house. I heard the gravel crunch as he pulled up, saw the car doors
open and their figures emerge in the half-light from the house
windows. I came out of the drawing room quietly and skulked in
the shadows of the little corridor leading to the cloakroom. My
parents and Uncle Affleck came downstairs from the parlour
where they had presumably been conferring; all of them looked
tense and strained. Imelda entered first. She was wrapped in a long
navy-blue winter coat and wore a red woollen scarf which accen-
tuated the extreme pallor of her face. Her eyes were huge and
oddly bright and she appeared desperately tired. Hubert followed,
looking worn and worried; as Imelda greeted the old people he
stood still on the threshold and rubbed his eyes wearily. Imelda
embraced my parents with unexpected warmth; but she seemed
oddly restrained as she rested her cheek on the breast of Uncle

Affleck; she allowed him to kiss her but seemed to be avoiding his intent gaze. Then she looked round with a vague, worried expression. 'Where is Frank?' I heard her ask, but no one bothered to reply. Little time was wasted on pleasantries and the whole party moved quickly upstairs. I emerged from my hiding-place as Restorick began bringing in the luggage. I was somewhat relieved to note that while Imelda seemed prepared for a long stay, Hubert had brought only one small suitcase.

Imelda did not appear at the dinner table that evening, but ate in her room. The atmosphere during the meal was fraught and jagged. Hubert was not, apparently, aware of the exact nature of Imelda's illness, but on the advice of her hosts and of their family doctor had acceded to her almost hysterical insistence that she be allowed to return to Lemington for a few weeks and to consult with Dr Downie, the Agnew family physician and a lifelong friend of Uncle Affleck. Hubert appeared profoundly depressed, which was not surprising, and showed extraordinary reluctance to discuss the matter at all. He insisted that he must return to Oxford within the next two or three days. My parents were naturally worried and puzzled; but I was particularly struck by the gloom and irritability of Uncle Affleck. He seemed on this occasion to have lost his natural superiority to events; he offered no advice on how best Imelda's nervous condition might be handled, answered questions snappishly and remained throughout dinner taciturn and moodily preoccupied.

Immediately after dinner, while the others were drinking their coffee, I slipped away upstairs, pretending that I was going to fetch a book. I was bent on a desperate course of action, but so distraught was my state of mind that I was willing to take any risk rather than remain ignorant of the truth. Knowing that I had little time to waste, I tore up the little stair leading to that part of the house where Uncle Affleck and Imelda had their rooms, and knocked urgently on the forbidden door.

'Imelda, my love! Open the door! It's me, Frank—I'm alone!'

Immediately I heard her cross the room with hurried footsteps; she turned the key and opened the door and almost threw herself into my arms.

'Oh, Superbo, my dearest, thank God you're here! But wait . . . are you sure no one has followed you?'

'I don't know—we'd better be quick—what's wrong, Imelda? Tell me what's wrong!'

Imelda stood back from me, but kept hold of my hands. She was pale and drawn, looked sick with worry, but there was a kind of bright, almost fevered animation in her eyes. She took a deep breath, then listened nervously for a moment or two before speaking, with passionate nervous energy.

'Frank, I am pregnant . . . and oh, Frank, Frank, the child is not, it is *not* Hubert's!'

I gasped with mingled astonishment, fear and pride as she clung to me again and laid her pure, pale face against my breast. I suppose that somewhere in my consciousness I must have been aware of such a possibility, but it had been thrust into the background by the fear of something much worse. I scarcely knew how to respond, but rocked her in my arms, making soothing, crooning sounds all the while and planting small, soft kisses all over her face, her hair and her neck.

'What are we going to do, Imelda?' was all I could think of saying. 'Dear God, what are we going to do?'

'I don't know. But we have this advantage: no one knows but you—you and the doctor in Oxfordshire. Hubert has been told only that I am severely debilitated, and that's the story he has passed on to your parents.'

'And Uncle Affleck?' I asked anxiously. 'You haven't told him?'

Imelda seemed almost to shudder at the thought of such an eventuality—one which would in the long run have to be faced up to. She sighed hopelessly and spoke in a whisper.

'Uncle Affleck . . . knows nothing.' Then she seemed seized by a sudden panic. 'Frank, you must go—go quickly, please. If you're found here, it will be utter disaster. Hubert will be gone in a couple of days, we'll have a chance to speak then. Please go, darling, I'm so frightened!'

I knew that she was right. I kissed her once again, with passionate abandon, and promised to work something out before we met again. As I stepped back to leave, my eye was caught by the little phial of snake venom still standing on the mantelpiece,

Imelda's emblem of man's triumph over the serpent. It seemed at once to mock and to accuse me. With the swiftness of light I flew back down the little stair and along the corridor towards my room. As I passed the head of the main staircase I saw below me Uncle Affleck coming up two steps at a time. He had not yet rounded the bend to face me, and I sped on and disappeared into my bedroom without his noticing me.

All that night, until three or four o'clock in the morning, I paced up and down in my room racking my brains for a solution. The situation in which we found ourselves was desperate, but not hopeless. If Imelda's marriage to Hubert could be prevented, there was a chance for us. From what Imelda had told me, it seemed clear that the child could not be Hubert's. When he discovered her pregnancy, it was possible that he might decide to end the engagement, but it was far more likely that he would not. Whatever his personal feelings might be—and it was already sufficiently clear that he was aware of our attachment and that it caused him great sorrow—there was no doubt that he deeply loved Imelda, and that his life was ruled by a rigorous code of honour and generosity. Like Uncle Affleck, he had a strong sense of the family and there could be little doubt that he would be under enormous pressure from Sir Robert and my parents to acknowledge the child as his, go ahead with the marriage as planned, suppress every hint of scandal and preserve unsullied the honour of the Agnews. As to Imelda, I could not feel confident, in spite of her great and undeniable love for me, that she would find the enormous resolution necessary to defy the wishes of the family and in particular those of Uncle Affleck, to whose will she had always been extraordinarily and doucely submissive. Least of all in her present situation would she be strongly placed to resist the temptation to accept Hubert and Lemington as father and ultimate home for her child, rather than risk the loss of all she had known and loved in order to make a hazardous and prospectless match with a disinherited outcast—which I could hardly doubt that I would be when the circumstances were known.

Were Imelda's marriage to Hubert somehow to become impossible, however, then there was a sporting chance that somehow or other *our* match might replace it. We might, and probably would, face violent family opposition; but when all was said and done, I was an Agnew and would be the father of Imelda's child. Her marriage to me might be considered preferable to the problems and the scandal arising from the birth of an illegitimate child, and the opprobrium that would attach to the family as well as to Imelda in that eventuality. Even were Uncle Agnew and my parents to prove inflexible, however (in my father's case I mean in effect, of course–to describe my progenitor as 'inflexible' would be like applying the adjective to a strand of chewed spaghetti), we could conceivably–Hubert being somehow out of the reckoning– go it alone.

But how on earth *could* Hubert be removed from the reckoning? One possibility which I considered carefully was a direct appeal to his better nature. Could he be persuaded that, Imelda being in love with me and about to become the mother of my child, natural justice demanded that he abdicate his position to myself? It was possible, but unlikely. I have to confess that he was not ungenerous, and that the jealousy which he presumably felt– and would doubtless feel more strongly when he learned of the pregnancy–would not be of the spiteful or resentful type. But two important and related factors would militate against his taking the hoped-for course of action. The first was his unswerving loyalty to Uncle Affleck, and the associated sense of family honour which he shared with Sir Robert. There could be no doubt that he would agree with Imelda's guardian that it was in her best interests and the family's that she should marry him and not me. And he would think so precisely because of the second factor, his well-known disapproval of myself and his undoubted conviction of my unsuitability to be Imelda's husband. I was well aware that, doubtless out of unacknowledged envy, he considered me to be immature and irresponsible. Even granted that he could isolate his own feelings from consideration of the issues, which was asking a lot from anyone, even the philosophical Yeti, I could have little confidence that his sense of rectitude would be overruled by the claims of my love and my dubious rights.

In the early hours I collapsed exhausted into bed, and during a few hours of deeply troubled sleep my worries were absorbed into the riot of my unconscious as I tossed and turned in a condition not far removed from delirium. I awoke feverish, and in some curious way distanced and abstracted from reality. I seemed to see everything through a kind of metaphysical fog, and I felt as if even the physical objects with which I came in contact were swathed in cotton wool. After breakfast–from which Imelda was again absent–I retired to my room and repeatedly played a record of Schubert's setting of Goethe's 'The Erlking', a song whose gloomy, haunting power accorded perfectly with my state of mind. I felt as if I were being driven helplessly forward by some invisible but all-compelling fate, but I did not understand how or whither. I was so agitated that I was unable to eat any lunch, and in the early afternoon I went out and began to wander haphazardly here and there about the wooded paths of Lemington.

The day was mild, but dark and full of foreboding, and a powerful wind was getting up–it felt as if a storm would soon break. Savage and incoherent gusts of wind were whipping the few remaining leaves off the trees and sending them packing here and there without discrimination in any direction, sucking them up towards the sky and spitting them back against my face; but high above, broken clouds tore across the sky in an endless, unflagging procession. The music of 'The Erlking' swept through my soul, and the image of the pursuing demon, relentlessly enticing the reluctant child from the charge of its fleeing father, took possession of my imagination. The spiritual atmosphere seemed charged with portent: something was being prepared up there for us here below–surely some revelation was at hand ...

In the rookery I came to a halt: a number of huge black birds were circling and cawing, cawing and circling–it appeared to me that they were waiting for something; there was an ominous sense of expectation; a great dark cloud was passing over the tops of the trees. Suddenly–out of the cloud, or so it seemed–a voice spoke, deep and clear and resonant:

'The Erlking' is a song by Schubert
Restorick must poison Hubert.

I felt no surprise: I gazed up at the cloud but could discern nothing, and the cloud passed on. I stood riveted to the spot, for I was sure that the voice would speak again. The black birds passed to and fro, cawing bleakly. I waited, unalarmed but expectant, my eyes fixed on the patch of sky above the tree from which the words had been spoken. After about a minute another huge, inky cloud swept towards the rookery; and as it passed overhead, once again that reverberating, potent, disembodied voice spoke from within its depths:

'The Erlking' is a song by Schubert
Restorick must poison Hubert.

So, the message remained the same. There was no longer any doubt: this voice, coming from outwith me, yet spoke within my own being, spoke the solution which my impotent will and my circumscribed understanding had been unable to encompass. It spoke with complete, unanswerable authority, and I did not attempt to argue with it. My time of inner turmoil and indecision was ended. The mental fog dispersed immediately from the doors of my perception, reality was again clear and palpable and distinct. I looked up once more to that speaking sky, and saw nothing but dashing cloud: only the wind spoke now its age-old untranslatable, unimaginable tongue. But I needed no further command: bafflement, soul-searching and procrastination were left behind, and I was full of energy and decision. I left the rookery without further delay and went off in search of Johnny Restorick. When I found him, I bribed him to perform the act that the voice had commanded. Since the onset of my mental illness a few months later, I have completely lost any recollection of actually doing so: I retain only the certain knowledge that I *did* do so. I do remember that later that afternoon the storm broke, and Lemington was battered all the rest of that day and all night by a tremendous tempest.

For the remainder of that day and the following day I remained, in contrast to the elements, calm and untroubled. It had been a Friday evening when Hubert and Imelda had arrived; Dr Downie was to come on Monday morning for a consultation with Imelda, and Hubert was to drive back to Oxford after the diagnosis had been made and future action discussed. The atmosphere in the house remained tense. Imelda remained in her room except for brief walks; when Hubert was with her he appeared to be solicitous but he was not unduly affectionate towards her. My father dithered around in a kind of submerged panic and my mother sighed much and looked martyred, as if Imelda's illness had been especially concocted in order to provide another cross for her to carry. As for Uncle Affleck, I had never seen him so nervous or so little in command of a situation. He was generally silent, but obviously found it difficult to keep still, fiddled around with the cutlery at meal times, and sometimes stood staring morosely out of the drawing room window for minutes at a time, quite abstracted from events around him. It was as if he, too, were waiting for something.

VI

On the Sunday night I went to bed early. My bedroom was next to Hubert's, and I heard him retire at about 11.30 p.m. I could not sleep; I was not restless or disturbed, but a sombre expectancy kept me wakeful, lying quietly listening to the gentle moaning of the fresh wind which had succeeded the earlier convulsion of nature. As I lay there, there were moments when I wanted to undo what I had done; but I was as powerless to undo it now as a man would be who had boarded the wrong train, and sought to regain his point of departure by walking back down the corridor, while even as he did so the train carried him forward to a destination that was unknown and undesired. At around one o'clock I heard Hubert belch loudly a number of times, then for a short space there was silence. When the eructations recommenced they were accompanied by the sounds of groaning, and sometimes sharper exclamations of distress. Then I heard Hubert go along the corridor to the bathroom, where he remained for quite some time. I began to grow tense: I could feel my feet sweating coldly beneath the sheets. After he had returned to his bedroom the groans grew louder and more unremitting, and at every moment I expected Hubert to knock at my door for assistance. But it was in consonance with his character, of course, to respond to his violent illness with foolhardy stoicism.

It must have been about half past two when Hubert let out
what I can only describe as a scream of agony. Every natural
human and brotherly impulse within me appealed to me to go to
him, but I steeled my will, and lay with my fists clenched,
drumming on the mattress with them and nervously wiggling my
sweaty toes. The horrific groaning continued for some minutes
longer, then I heard Hubert open the door once more. I leapt out
of bed and went out to the corridor. He was leaning doubled up
in agony against the wall, his face the colour of dirty linen and the
sweat pouring from his brow.

"Frank!" he gasped, "doctor . . . quick . . . no, no . . .
ambulance!"

I made to assist him and take him back to his room, but he
waved me violently away.

"No, no! Doctor . . . ambulance . . . quickly!"

I dashed off in the direction of the phone, but when I reached
the hall waited for five or ten minutes longer before calling Dr
Downie. At every moment I had to struggle not to lift the
receiver, and to prevent myself doing so prematurely I even
went into the library and turned over unseeingly a few pages of
Thucydides. When I did get through to the sleepy physician I had
to judge my message very delicately. I impressed upon him that
Hubert was severely ill and that I was sure a visit was really
necessary, but I took care not to make the situation sound so
grave that Dr Downie would insist on my phoning at once for an
ambulance. He promised to arrive within twenty minutes, and I
then went to rouse my parents. When we reached Hubert's room
he was lying prone on the floor just inside the door. An appalling
stench filled the room, issuing from a pile of bloody vomit in the
washhand basin. He proved too heavy for us to lift and my father
dashed off for Uncle Affleck. With the latter's assistance we
managed to raise the poor Yeti and lay him on the bed. He was
unconscious, his freckled face was a ghastly white and the sweat
still glistened on his brow; his breathing was shallow and his pulse
extremely slow and weak.

Satisfied of the existence of a crisis, Uncle Affleck had regained
on the instant his full executive powers. Indeed he was magnificent to behold, striding purposefully about the room in his

splendid silk dressing-gown, issuing orders and marvellously
calming my near-hysterical mother. When at one point Hubert
appeared to have stopped breathing, the latter was pathetically
anxious to try artificial respiration, but Uncle Affleck imperiously
forbade the attempt, adducing some cogent medical arguments on
the possible dangers of the procedure for one in Hubert's particular condition. When Dr Downie arrived he took one look at
the patient and ordered an ambulance to be called without delay.
Uncle Affleck snapped his fingers at me and pointed in the direction of the door. Ordinarily I would have told him to do the job
himself, but I had my own reasons for wanting an excuse to leave.

I quickly made the call and then dashed off to Imelda, who had
not been wakened. I passed Uncle Affleck's open bedroom door,
knocked loudly and rapidly several times on Imelda's, went in
without waiting for her response and switched on the light.
Imelda raised herself on her elbow, drugged with sleep and
squinting against the light. Her hair was ruffled, her face
beguilingly pale; her pyjama jacket was half open, showing the
curve of a pure white breast, and a golden crucifix hung at her
neck.

"Imelda!" I cried, "it's w . . . we can . . . Hubert's desperately
ill! I'm not sure if he's going to live!"

Imelda gasped in horror and raised her hands to her mouth. For
a moment or two she sat there in bed as if paralysed, then she
pushed back the bedclothes and jumped to the floor. She stood for
an instant gazing at me, then looked down at herself: her pyjama
trousers were soaked with urine and clinging to her thighs. So
that had started again—a recurrence was always a sure sign of
mental distress! Imelda grimaced and reached for her dressing-
gown to cover her shame.

"What's wrong with him?" she asked as we hurried downstairs,
"what's happened?"

"I think his ulcer's burst . . . Oh, Imelda, perhaps we can be
together after all!"

"Frank, Frank! How can you say such a thing now? I've had
such awful thoughts myself, almost wished that this might
happen, his stomach's been so bad recently . . . oh God, I feel as
if I'd willed death on him!"

When we arrived at the sick chamber they were all standing numbed and silent, in utter shock, even the doctor: my brother showed no sign of life. Before the ambulance arrived Dr Downie had pronounced him dead. I broke down and wept. I shall not attempt to describe the harrowing scenes of grief and distress which followed. For my parents, it was the beginning of the end. My father never recovered from his bereavement, and was to die, a broken man, less than two years later; my mother followed him after a similar interval. Imelda, the overwhelming shock of the event altogether too much for her in her delicate condition, fainted on the spot and was carried back to bed by Uncle Affleck and Dr Downie. (Though in my wildest forebodings I could not have conceived of the possibility at the time, I was never to see her again.) I was myself in a condition of potential hysteria, the accumulated strains and tensions of the preceding months, now released by so violent a catastrophe, stretching to the utmost the powers of a constitution naturally tough and resilient.

At this hour of familial devastation, Uncle Affleck alone was a very rock of strength and endurance. Heroically mastering his overwhelming grief at the loss of his adored protégé and the ruin of his dynastic ambitions, he manfully shouldered the burden of attending to all the myriad practicalities relating to a bereavement, a task of which my father was utterly incapable, and at the same time expended his tireless energies on comforting the rest of us and generally ensuring that life went on in spite of the devastating loss of the one in whom all the family's hopes and aspirations had been so misguidedly placed. Uncle Affleck it was, too, who inadvertently saved my skin by persuading Dr Downie that a post-mortem was utterly unnecessary and would only add to the pain and distress of the family at this sorrowful time. Hubert had been under treatment for his ulcer for years, and so severe and debilitating had his condition been in recent months that at the time of his death he was awaiting an appointment for a consultation with yet another specialist on his return to Oxford. In such circumstances Dr Downie had no difficulty in filling in the cause of death on the death certificate as peritonitis resulting from a perforated duodenal ulcer. The rapidity with which death had ensued was due, the doctor was convinced, to shock.

But was Uncle Affleck's intervention so entirely fortuitous? It was natural that in the days between Hubert's decease and the funeral I was constantly on the look-out for Johnny Restorick. I wanted to find out from him with what concoction he had carried out my wishes, and how it had been introduced. I needed the companionship and sense of fellow-feeling that can only be had from one's co-conspirator; above all I wanted to be reassured that our secret was safe, that Restorick would not, in some manner which I could not anticipate, betray me. I was in fact desperate to find him, but though I searched high and low no Johnny was to be found. In the circumstances I did not dare to make inquiries, and no one else at the time was in the slightest interested in the tinker's whereabouts. It was only some days after the funeral that Uncle Affleck announced that his body-servant had been dismissed as a result of yet another scandal in the village. This time, he averred, Restorick had tried his patience too far; under great strain as a result of Hubert's death, he had flown off the handle when learning of the tinker's latest misdeeds and had ordered him to leave Lemington forthwith, never to return.

It could not fail to occur to me that Uncle Affleck might have got wind of his ex-batman's part in the death of his favoured 'son', perhaps even by Restorick's own confession. In that case the overwhelming likelihood must be that he would have given him up to the police; but on the other hand, it *was* conceivable that the combination of Uncle Affleck's extreme horror at the possibility of family scandal, and his own disgracefully intimate relations with his servant, might have stayed his hand and persuaded him to the banishment of Restorick rather than his denouncement. In that case, did Uncle Affleck know also of *my* initiating and commanding role in the murderous operation?

Such a possibility could not fail to fill me with horror. Was my uncle keeping back his information until it could be used against me to the greatest advantage and the most devastating effect? If Uncle Affleck did have any such hold over me, it must be said that he never, either in his words or by his attitude, gave me even the slightest hint of it. It is altogether more likely that Restorick—enriched, of course, by my substantial bribe—fled of his own accord to make a new life elsewhere; and that Uncle Affleck, too proud to admit that he knew nothing about his long-time servant and henchman's disappearance, but no doubt suspecting that it indicated nothing good, hit upon the most obvious and plausible explanation for public consumption. So far as I am aware, nothing has ever been seen or heard of Johnny Restorick since that time. But though my reason sought to persuade me that the scenario arrived at above was the true one, the horrid possibility of my secret being in Uncle Affleck's keeping and my future utterly in his power lay always at the back of my mind, like a fearful spectre housed in some back room which I dare not enter, and I have no doubt that this repressed but unremitting terror contributed substantially to my mental collapse a few months later.

The funeral was held in the Episcopalian church of which my father was rector, on the morning of the fourth day after Hubert's decease. My father felt incapable of conducting the service, though he was determined to assist; the task was undertaken by an old friend of his whom he had known in Edinburgh, one Father Goodlad. Imelda was not present, remaining in her room in a condition of near-collapse; Dr Downie was professedly deeply worried about her state of health, though it was not clear to me at the time whether or not he was yet aware of her pregnancy. Because of my father's role in the funeral service it once again fell on Uncle Affleck to assume on this sad day the position of head of the family. Beautifully turned out in the old style, he was a commanding and a comforting presence, a rock for the grieving mother to lean upon, an embodied symbol of the family, of its solidarity and its will to continuity in the face of tragedy and adversity. Yet I could not help feeling that there was something oddly inappropriate to the occasion in his demeanour, something that I found it difficult to put my finger on until a memory flashed upon me of the obsequies of old Wing Commander. As Father Goodlad raised his hand in the final blessing, I momentarily expected Uncle Affleck to respond with the Nazi salute.

Father Goodlad was a large, robust, bespectacled man of about fifty, with an air of certainty, of determination, perhaps even a shade of truculence. When my father broke down sobbing in the middle of a sequence of prayers, Father Goodlad took over efficiently and without ceremony, calling out the intercessions in

a loud, booming voice and transforming the whole tenor from my
father's broken submissiveness to a tone of hope and confidence:
one could almost, indeed, have detected a hint of *defiance* in his
attitude. His encomium of Hubert's qualities had something quite
disturbing about it. Hubert was the kind of young man, he
declared, whose very modesty and self-effacement, whose lack of
self-assertion and whose kindly tolerance, could arouse fierce
resentment and even jealousy in those of an opposite temperament, and especially in those less gifted with natural endowments.
While elaborating this point at some length, he stared hard and
coldly at myself: I had never met Father Goodlad in my life, yet
the implication was unmistakable. Sometimes he actually paused
and gazed at me with his thick, bushy, reddish eyebrows slightly
raised in a schoolmasterly way, as if detecting insubordination. It
was a most upsetting experience.

After the service a small sherry reception was held at
Lemington. From across the drawing room I could see Father
Goodlad once again directing at me his cold, unflinching glower.
Considerably unnerved yet determined to get to the bottom of his
attitude towards me, I boldly went across to him, offered him my
hand (which he took somewhat reluctantly, I thought), and
thanked him sincerely though not over-effusively for the spirit in
which he had conducted the funeral. He answered more or less
monosyllabically, gazing at me with an air of slight but unmistakable distaste. By now thoroughly embarrassed and put out, I
began, for want of anything better to say, to blurt out an account
of the present state of my mycological studies. His tangled
eyebrows rose far above the upper rim of his glasses, and his face
assumed an amused, quizzical and disdainful expression. But I
could scarcely believe the evidence of my senses when, after
muttering something incomprehensible to himself, he laid his
glass down on a table and actually walked off while I was still
speaking to him. Such discourtesy must have some very definite
meaning, and Father Goodlad's unaccountable behaviour threw
me into a state of extreme nervous turmoil. Yet before he left
he came over to me, shook my hand, looked me straight in
the eye, and remarked, with every appearance of sincerity, 'I shall
pray for you.' Then, when he was already outside the door, he

came back in, leaned towards me and said loudly, "We shall meet again, I'm sure." A huge hand raised in general farewell, and he was gone.

About a week after the funeral, the further blow long awaited by myself but totally unsuspected by the rest of the family, fell upon the house of Agnew. One morning Dr Downie asked to see Uncle Affleck privately and informed him, as Imelda's guardian, that his ward was pregnant. Sir Robert, sombre but controlled, made the announcement at lunch-time. It was received, of course, in a quite different frame of mind from that which would have prevailed had Hubert been alive. In one sense his decease made the matter more serious, because if he had lived the pair could have married long before the birth, thus neutralising to at least some extent the situation's worst potential for shame and scandal. On the other hand, my parents would have been quite inhuman if they had not experienced a measure of joy at the thought that Hubert would now–as they naturally believed–leave behind him some offspring to perpetuate his memory and continue the line, marred though it might be by a bar sinister. So the tears that fell were extraordinarily mixed and ambiguous in their significance. To my considerable surprise, the whole matter was discussed and dissected quite openly in front of me. Various competing solutions to the problem were canvassed and arguments for and against tossed to and fro, but in the end Uncle Affleck was insistent that nothing could be decided upon except with the consent and co-operation of Imelda herself.

He spent all that afternoon closeted with her. I was of course wildly on edge, imaging to myself every possible scenario that might ensue when Imelda revealed her child's true paternity. I was frightened, excited, determined and aggressive by turns. I visualised appalling reactions of fury from Uncle Affleck, saw myself break into my love's room by force and remove her somehow from his wardance, heard the supplications of my parents and their pleas to Uncle Agnew that we be allowed to marry and remain at Lemington with our child, its future inheritor; I imagined Imelda torn between her love for me and her loyalty to her guardian, saw her sink to her knees before both of us begging that we be reconciled, swearing on Hubert's dead

bones that he had already purposed to resign his place in
her affections to myself. All afternoon I strode in tremendous
agitation along the paths that the three of us had frequented in
days gone by, conjuring up before my eyes such terrific scenes of
emotional crisis and conflict. The reality proved vastly different.

Uncle Affleck reappeared at tea-time looking relaxed and com-
fortable with himself. He settled himself deep in his armchair as
my mother poured the tea, and placed his finger-tips together as
he had done during the 'family conference'. I waited in desperate
anticipation for the bombshell to be dropped, but nothing of that
nature happened at all. Even from his preliminary remarks it was
immediately apparent that nothing had occurred to disturb the
established assumption that the expected child was Hubert's.
Imelda had betrayed me! Faced by so fearful a prospect as that
promised by her guardian's opinion of myself, grief-stricken,
guilty, drained and confused, she had taken the line of least
resistance and had not dared to tell him the truth. With Hubert no
longer there to deny it, must it not have seemed welcome to the
morally and physically exhausted girl to sink into the warm
protecting bosom of the family, to go along with its established
expectations and its desires, rather than to risk casting in her lot
with its outcast and rejected son—as I certainly would be when the
truth were known, even if I were not quite that already? I could
not blame her, but my hurt and my bafflement went too deep for
words.

Yet was there not another possible explanation? Perhaps Imelda
had told Uncle Affleck the truth, but he had persuaded her that it
was in the best interests of all that it should remain a secret to my
parents, and formally at least to myself. It was impossible to
overestimate the possible extent of Sir Robert's influence over his
ward. But even if she had been disposed to protest, her capacity
for resistance must be limited. I had sometimes wondered during
the past days to what extent Imelda's seclusion was voluntary; at
times I had the feeling that she was being kept a virtual prisoner
in her room. Perhaps Uncle Affleck was simply determined to
impose his will on the poor girl at whatever cost to her happiness
and by whatever means were at his disposal.

Yet I had to admit to myself that if he knew the truth about the child's paternity, even if he were determined to keep it from my parents, it was highly unlikely that some indication of it would not have surfaced in his attitude to myself. He might be a good actor and he might be playing a clever game, but there were limits even to Uncle Affleck's powers of dissimulation. On the contrary, it seemed to me that since Hubert's death his feelings towards me had appreciably and genuinely softened. It might be that he was gradually acclimatising himself to the prospect that I might eventually replace my brother in his affectionate regard; if that should be the case, I must on no account upset the possibility by antagonising him, for in that eventuality lay by far the best hope for Imelda's ultimate happiness and my own.

'Imelda feels,' said Uncle Affleck, 'that it is too early yet for her to decide whether or not she should keep the child. On the whole I agree with her.'

'Oh, but Robert!' cried my mother in great alarm, 'she must! The child is Hubert's—it will be our grandchild! You're surely not suggesting that she should give it away?'

'At the moment, my dear,' said Uncle Affleck imperturbably, 'I am suggesting nothing. I am proposing merely that nothing be decided yet. We shall let matters take their natural course—the final decision must naturally be Imelda's. But one thing I do feel quite strongly about—and Imelda agrees with me entirely: she should not remain at Lemington while she is awaiting the birth. In the first place: well, Berkwickshire is still a narrow-minded place. There would be talk, let's not doubt that, and while it would be of no real significance, it would still be unpleasant for Imelda, not to speak of the rest of us. More importantly, though, much more importantly, we have to think of this. Lemington is full of memories for Imelda—memories that at such a time can't fail to make her unhappy. She would be far better off back at Charlton-on-Otmoor, where she has good friends and will be well cared for, where she can look forward instead of backwards, where she can set about building herself a new life. After the baby is born, of course . . . the decision will be hers,' he summed up, conclusively, and waited for their response.

'Dear, dear,' said my father plaintively. 'Oh, dear, dear.' But my mother nodded her head slowly. She could see the force of these arguments, and no mistake: especially the first of them. As for me, I was utterly aghast. While they were still talking I slipped out of the room and dashed off to Imelda's. I knocked violently on the door, shouted out her name and rattled the handle: it was locked.

'Go away, Frank!' she cried urgently from within, 'please go away! I can't speak to you. It's all over–there's nothing you can do. Please, Frank, please, for both of our sakes! And for the baby's too! Don't stay, Uncle Affleck will kill you! Oh, I can't bear this!' I heard muffled sobbing and imagined that she had thrown herself on the bed.

'Imelda! This is frightful! My darling, for God's sake open the door! It's me, Frank, don't you understand? You can't let them do this to us! Oh, Imelda!'

So it went on for some time, and all to no avail. After a time she answered no more, and I was speaking only to a palpable, stubborn silence. My spirit drooped, my will slackened, a tremendous weariness enveloped my body. I hesitated a moment, opened my mouth once more and shut it again; then I turned and left. I had had my last contact with my beloved Imelda.

A few days later Imelda and Uncle Affleck left Lemington under cover of darkness. I remained in my room but I heard them go. Uncle Affleck took Imelda to Oxfordshire, remained a few days and, I believe, returned. The following day I myself departed and went to stay with a friend in Edinburgh. I wrote to Imelda at Charlton-on-Otmoor on three occasions but received no reply. By the time her baby was born in June my reason had given way, and I had been sectioned under the Mental Health Act and incarcerated in the Royal Edinburgh Hospital. Following the birth, as I later learned, Imelda returned with our daughter to Lemington and stayed for about a week. The baby was given into the care of a childless couple who lived in one of the farm cottages; I believe the husband was a tractorman. Later they adopted her and left the district. I learned of this only recently, by a very circuitous route. I am convinced that the loss of their grandchild contributed to the premature deaths of my parents. After giving her child up, Imelda left immediately for the south of England and never returned.

VII

On the departure of Imelda I decided to settle in Edinburgh for a while. During the past years I had made rather frequent trips there in connection with my mycological studies, and quite often I would stay over for a few nights. At first my acquaintance had been more or less limited to old school friends, but gradually I had become intimate with a wider circle, and now had several buddies on whom I could rely for hospitality. There was absolutely nothing to keep me at Lemington, where I was tortured by memories which had now become miserable and assailed by darts of conscience which threatened the pursuit of avenging Furies. I took a bedsitter in the flat of a friend at the eastern end of the New Town, and in a desperate, almost panic-stricken effort to forget Imelda and to push back the full consciousness of what I had done, I plunged into a life of wild carousal and alcoholic excess.

I had been in Edinburgh only for a day or two when I first saw Father Goodlad. It was in a dingy second-hand bookshop where I was filling in time until the pubs opened. I was leafing over some dusty tome in a shadowy corner when the door opened with a peremptory rattle and the big, robust priest burst into the shop. He strode unhesitatingly towards the theology section and at once began rummaging among the shelves, pulling books out, thumbing through a few pages noisily and ostentatiously in a way which could not possibly have allowed him to take any cognisance of the contents, and then tossing them back impatiently into their places. Whatever he was looking for, he was evidently frustrated in his search. I was eyeing him gingerly, ready to drop my eyes hurriedly to my volume if he showed any sign of looking in my direction. But quite suddenly he did so, not in the least as if by chance, but rather as if he had known all along that I was there, and had even come into the bookshop expressly to deliver at me this panoptic and withering glance. I almost felt myself cringe and shrink protectively within myself: if I had had a shell I would certainly have disappeared altogether inside it.

'So,' said Father Goodlad, not loudly but with awful distinctness, 'we meet again.' He nodded to himself several times while continuing to gaze at me coldly yet impassively; then he turned on his heel without further ado and strode out of the shop.

During the next few weeks, in the most unexpected places, I had a number of further and similar encounters with the ominous cleric. Sometimes I saw him without his appearing to see me, at other times the same unpleasant and unsettling eye contact took place between us. I had heard that Edinburgh was a place where certain kenspeckle characters could be seen almost daily, but generally these were to be found on predictable beats at definite times of day. Father Goodlad, however, had a disturbing habit of turning up wherever I happened to be, and before long I began to feel persecuted and pursued. After the initial meeting he never spoke to me; until, that is, the occasion of our final and decisive encounter.

One Friday night I was drinking in a pub called the Nor' Loch with a group of people who included my friend Wee Tam, who worked in the antiquarian bookshop above mentioned, and his girlfriend Jenny. By about ten o'clock our little fellowship had already passed well beyond moderation. All thoughts of a mid-evening break to visit the Little Friar fish bar across the road, or the Good Luck Chinese carry-out down the hill, had now been forgotten. Raucous singing had begun, and at one point, I remember, Wee Tam stood briefly on a chair and tried to perform a song of his own composition about Scotch pies. It was at that point that, with a certain unfocussed astonishment and a great sinking of the heart, I observed Father Goodlad among the throng, swinging his whisky glass with vigorous appreciation. At our table there were displays of bravado and scurrility, dirty stories were told, vulgar laughter was heard and the general standard of our behaviour deteriorated rapidly. Father Goodlad, who for some reason was hanging about in our vicinity, was in this respect as gross an offender as anyone. When Tam got up to buy a round of drinks the priest even started dummy-boxing with him, bobbing and weaving and making as if to prevent Tam getting to the bar. I frowned angrily at this unseemly display.

'Would you look at that degenerate cleric,' I remarked to Tam as he returned with the drinks. 'I've seldom seen such reprehensible conduct.'

'Have to humour him,' explained Tam sagely. 'Wan o' wur best customers.'

'Yes, I saw him in the shop a couple of weeks ago.'

'There's nae herm in him,' replied Tam inconsequently. 'It's good to see him enjoying himself. Nae herm in him.' He seemed evasive, even a little secretive.

Everything that happened that night is for some reason etched on my memory with almost preternatural clarity, although the quantity of drink which I had consumed ought to have produced quite the opposite effect. Wee Tam got up again, this time to visit the lavatory, and emboldened by alcohol I am afraid I took advantage of his temporary absence by nuzzling Jenny's neck and slipping my hand under her blouse. It meant absolutely nothing, of course, and I am glad to say that Jenny, evidently in no mood for such endearments, firmly repelled my advances. But what was my horror when, looking up in shamefaced defeat, I beheld only a few feet away the outraged Father Goodlad, directing upon me a most terrifying look of thunderous rebuke! The brows of the gigantic priest were corrugated, his eyes flashed coruscating fire, his gaze was undeviating, remorseless, utterly condemnatory! All the unfitting foolery in which he had been indulging had fallen away from him in an instant: now he was Justice personified, and I quailed before him and hung my hand in mute acceptance of the towering reprimand.

I was utterly unnerved. My first impulse was to get another drink, in fact a large whisky, and I got up and began to push my way, no doubt rather rudely, towards the bar. The faces that turned towards me were all hostile, ugly and distorted, the features bulbous and bloated, the eyes flashing a dull contempt, the mouths twisted and sneering: nightmare figures out of Hieronymus Bosch. I began to feel faint, the clammy sweat broke out on my brow, and forgetting the thought of a drink I made my way to the toilet and weakly splashed my face with cold water. Exhausted and shaking, I leaned against the wall: a man stared at me with unsympathetic aversion, no doubt assessing me, as I imagined with shame, as just another poor sod who couldnae hold his drink.

When I had recovered a little from my faintness I began to

work my way back towards my seat, but alas, between myself and the table stood the terrible Father Goodlad, observing my approach with a determined eye. I attempted to take a roundabout route, but the dreadful priest moved stealthily but swiftly to bar my way. Placing an iron hand on my shoulder he held me in a deadly grip: I stared mesmerised at the tangled reddish hair in his broad nostrils. 'Uriah the Hittite!' he said, in a tone which could not be evaded; then he moved his face closer to mine and whispered in my ear, slowly and with awful distinctness, 'You are the man.'

I had no need to ask what he meant. The story of David and Bathsheba and her husband Uriah the Hittite had been known to me since childhood—how vividly I recalled, at that moment, a relentless sermon on this very text, an eloquent and fearsome warning of the murderous lengths to which a man might be brought by passion and adultery! Now the whispered words of the priest burst asunder the bonds of repression in which I had enchained my conscience, and guilt flashed in my heart; it was as if those words had exploded in the hidden depths of my own psyche and set off a fire-storm in my mind. I had to leave, and struggled towards the door with a gait that felt broken and hunched. My eyes swept the bar for a sign of Father Goodlad, but he was nowhere to be seen.

The next afternoon, nursing the stubborn remains of a raging hangover, my spirit suffused with a sickness of shame and guilt, I pulled down from a shelf the old Bible of my childhood, which I still took with me wherever I went, and turned to the Second Book of Samuel, the eleventh chapter, at the second verse. I did not in the least want to do so, but the words of Father Goodlad had spoken themselves deep in my soul and willy-nilly they compelled me to read. There was a masochism about it, too. I wanted to torture myself with the truth, to taste my own foulness. I wanted to know my sin, to savour its darkness, flagellate myself with its lacerating, knotted cords. This was the story that I read.

King David was walking on the roof of his house one fine afternoon and he saw a beautiful woman bathing. He inquired who she was, and was told that she was Bathsheba the wife of Uriah the Hittite. 'So David sent messengers, and took her; and she came to him, and he lay with her.' And not long afterwards she sent him word that she was with child. So David sent for Uriah, who had been away fighting David's war, and attempted by guile to get him to go home and sleep with his wife. But Uriah, knowing that his commander Joab and his comrades were sleeping in the open fields, knew that it would be dishonourable for him to do so, and he refused. Then David sent a letter to Joab, saying, 'Set Uriah in the forefront of the hardest fighting, and then draw back from him, that he may be struck down, and die.' And that was how it turned out. Bathsheba lamented for her husband, but when the mourning was over David took her as his wife and she bore him a son. 'But the thing that David had done displeased the Lord.'

Then the Lord sent Nathan the prophet to David with a parable, about a rich man with abundant flocks and herds, and a poor man with only one little ewe lamb to which he was so devoted that it was like a daughter to him. The rich man, having a wayfarer to entertain, was unwilling to take one of his own flock to prepare for eating and took the poor man's lamb instead. David was enraged when he heard the story; but Nathan told him, 'You are the man . . . You have smitten Uriah the Hittite with the sword, and have taken his wife to be your wife, and have slain him with the sword of the Amorites.' David confessed his sin against the Lord. The Lord had put away his sin, Nathan told him, and he would not die. Nevertheless, because he had scorned the Lord, the child born to him would die. And that was how it turned out. David prayed and fasted and wept for the child while it was sick, but when it died he arose, washed, anointed himself, dressed and worshipped in the house of the Lord; then he went home and had a meal. 'Then David comforted his wife, Bathsheba, and went in to her, and lay with her, and she bore a son, and he called his name Solomon. And the Lord loved him . . .'

I sat with the Bible on my knee and stared desolately ahead of me at the seasonal nakedness which had overtaken the little garden without. The message for me at the heart of the story was not to be evaded: 'You are the man.' There was nothing to be said about it, no excuse to be made, no justification to be prepared. I was the man. Hubert was Uriah, was the poor man, so much less

richly endowed than myself with every advantage bestowed by
nature, who had only his one ewe lamb Imelda to give him
comfort. I had stolen his ewe lamb and had put him to death with
the sword of the Amorites, with the poison of Restorick. And if
Hubert were indeed Uriah the Hittite, as Father Goodlad averred,
who was that terrible priest himself? Who but Nathan the
prophet; and therefore one sent by the Lord? One sent to warn me
that unless I repented my sin, the vengeance of God would soon
pursue me . . .

Who was this man who had so suddenly yet stealthily entered
my life, who seemed in a strange way always to have known me,
though until the day of Hubert's funeral I had never met him? Or
had I? Was there not, when I came to give it thought, something
elusively familiar about that truculent priest? Father Goodlad had
told me that day that we would meet again, and we had; but was
there not also, in the manner of his intonation, a suggestion that
we had also met before? In spite of the terror which his appearances
and his message inspired in me, I yet had the sense that he was not
in the final analysis hostile to the salvation of my soul. In the story
of David and Bathsheba and Uriah the Hittite there was, as well
as a tremendous warning of God's power and wrath, a breath of
hope, which came fleetingly upon me like the first faint stirring
of a gentle breeze: 'And she bore a son, and he called his
name Solomon. And the Lord loved him.' For Solomon was
Wisdom: out of folly and wickedness and scorn of God was
born Wisdom.

But between myself and Wisdom was yet a great gulf fixed.
Before I could even hope to turn towards her, I had first to
descend into the hell of madness and spiritual destitution. The
onset of my rapid and almost complete mental collapse occurred
within a few days of Father Goodlad's final visitation. Of that
calamity I can remember almost nothing. With my eventual, and
only partial, emergence from this nightmare a new story begins.
The present story is ended.

Imelda, my heart, my soul, beautiful, bright, destroying angel,
where are you now? Forgive me if you can. I played my part in
your ruin as you did in mine. I think of our child sometimes—the
child I never saw—where is *she*? Should she ever read this I ask for

her forgiveness too, and for her prayers: for you, for me, for Hubert, for all of us. Imelda, goodbye.

Memoir Of Sir Robert Affleck

I am asked to give some account of the Agnew family of Lemington from the time when I became a 'resident member', as it were, in the year 1950, until its dispersal following the tragic death of my nephew Hubert Agnew late in 1962. It is a heavy undertaking, for of the six people who made up our family group at that time, four are now dead and one is permanently incarcerated in a mental hospital. I alone survive with my faculties intact, but I am an old, sad and weary man. In such circumstances even happy memories– by which I mean memories of events which were in themselves, and at the time, happy–become unbearably painful; but by no means all the memories of those years come into that category. On the contrary: very few of them do. In retrospect it seems to me that all that period of my life was overshadowed by the cloud of coming disaster. But for the sake of future historians of that ancient and once distinguished house, I shall not shirk my task.

It is necessary first to explain my circumstances at the time when I came to live at Lemington. Briefly then. Since the conclusion of my war service I had been very contentedly employed in factoring the large estate of Salachy in Wester Ross. I loved the people there and their way of life, and had no other thought than to spend the rest of my days in those remote fastnesses, far removed from the cheapness and the vulgarity of what, lamentably, passes today for 'civilisation'. But it was not to be. In the summer of 1949 I had to go to Nigeria to collect a poor little orphan who had become my responsibility and who had no one else to care for her. Imelda Cranstoun was the daughter of my cousin Isobel Affleck, who had married a Church of Scotland missionary. Early in 1949 he had perished from snakebite; and within a few months of his death Isobel followed him to the grave, the victim of some obscure and never confidently identified tropical illness. At that date the little Imelda was not quite eight years-old. I shall never forget the first time that I laid eyes on her, a tiny, fragile creature with huge grey eyes, holding onto the hand of her black nanny. When I had bent down and introduced myself to her and spoken a few kind words, she said:

"You will be my Daddy now, Uncle Affleck . . . but who will be my Mummy?"

The poor child's words were frequently on my mind during the year which followed. I took her back with me to Salachy, but Imelda was unsettled and disturbed, and because I had no wife to care for her my task was a far from easy one. Fortunately, it was not long before what seemed to be an ideal solution presented itself. Since not long after he had inherited the Lemington estate, my brother-in-law Charles Agnew had been largely occupied in studying for the Episcopalian priesthood. The estate had fallen into the hands of an unscrupulous agent, an accomplished rogue who was filching it of thousands of pounds a year under the very nose of its unworldy laird. It had previously been suggested that I should come to Berwickshire to sort out the appalling mess which had resulted and to take over the management. I had at first refused the offer, preferring to remain where I was, but now my sister, knowing how deeply concerned I was about the mother-less state of my little Imelda, pressed me to come and live at Lemington so that she might share with me the parental role. In the circumstances, it was impossible for me to refuse.

Imelda and I arrived at Lemington in September 1950. My sister made us both wonderfully welcome, and in the years to come she was, I venture to assert, a more caring and devoted mother to my little orphan than many a natural mother would have been. Poor Charles also did his best, but the truth is that he was utterly unfitted to be a family man. Scholarly, retiring and quite ineffectual, he had already virtually abdicated responsibility for the training and upbringing of his two sons. The result was that I found myself obliged to assume a role as substitute father which I neither sought nor desired, but which otherwise would have gone by default. Indeed, I have no doubt that my dear sister had the needs of her own boys in mind, as well as those of Imelda, when she persuaded me to come to Lemington. I am aware that in some respects I did not make a very good job of it, but in my own defence I must point out that one half of the material was already irremediably spoilt.

The two boys could scarcely have afforded a more striking contrast. Hubert, the elder, at that time ten and a half years old, was a sturdy, fun-loving little redhead. Without being pushy or over-talkative, he was excitedly keen to show Imelda everything in the house and policies, to welcome her and make her feel at home. He had a touching instinctive feeling for the needs of the shy, lonely child thrust suddenly into an environment that was utterly strange to her and into the company of a whole group of unfamiliar faces. Nothing of the sort could be said of Frank, who at nine was just the same age as Imelda. Emotionally, one would have placed him as two or three years younger than that. He was that kind of sickly, whining, plaintive child so aptly characterised by the fine old Scots expression 'a girny bairn'. How unlike his brother! Not for him all the natural rough-and-tumble of a healthy country boyhood. He was always skulking about by himself with his hands in his pockets, idly kicking pine cones or bits of wood, or else lying on the floor in the library wasting his time on the romantic fantasisings of long outdated literature.

Although at first seemingly resentful of what he thought of as Imelda's intrusion into his jealously-guarded private world, Frank soon became fascinated with his second cousin in the way in which some boys do who—unable to get on with contemporaries of their own sex because of their shrinking timidity—seek the less exacting and demanding ambience of female company. So he began to hang onto the coat-tails of Hubert—with whom he had nothing in common, and, up till then, had had very little to do—simply because Hubert was Imelda's natural companion in quite a different way: her leader, her guide in a new and strange and exciting world; her protector and potentially her beau. It was during the long summer holidays that the three of them spent most time together, for by the time of our arrival at Lemington both boys were already at boarding-school.

Here let me say that it is a matter of great regret to me that I could not make similar arrangements for Imelda's education. There was a good reason for not doing so, however: she was enuretic, a condition which had come upon her following the shock of losing both her parents within a few months. This being the case it seemed to me, knowing the distress which her weakness already caused her, that it would have been needlessly cruel to have taken that course of action. To have sent such a shy and sensitive child to the rough-and-ready local school was, I felt at the time, equally unthinkable. Imelda was therefore schooled at home, and in strictly educational terms the results were no cause for regret. However, the unavoidable lack of friends of her own age meant that she was entirely dependent for companionship upon the two Agnew boys, and grew up in an unhealthy hothouse atmosphere. Had there been only Hubert, all would have been well, for he and Imelda were a pair so obviously made for each other; Frank was the snake in the grass, if I may be permitted the expression. Where males and females are concerned, whatever their age, three is a bad number; I was aware of that at the time, but a remedy was not readily to be found.

I should, I know, have been impartial in my attitude to the two brothers, but I confess that I found it impossible. When the one was a good-natured, healthy-minded, clean-living, uncomplicated specimen, intelligent and hard-working but at the same time unpretentious and naturally modest about his considerable abilities; and the other was a conceited pup, weak-willed and unmanly but inordinately inflated in his conception of his own powers, given to ridiculous airs and graces, whingeing and self-pitying when crossed or checked; in such circumstances impartiality proved no easy matter. And I have to confess that I harboured a special little hope that one day Hubert and Imelda would realise that their affection for each other was one which would last a lifetime, that they would marry and raise a family, and in the happiest possible way tie the fortunes of the Agnews and the Afflecks yet more closely together.

Hubert was the heir to Lemington—who more suited to be its mistress than Imelda? As they grew into their teens it became increasingly plain that that beautiful bright angel felt herself irresistibly drawn to the splendid young fellow. Yet women are notoriously unpredictable creatures; and there was Frank, always hanging about, as it were, in the wings, the understudy living for the day when the principal player would for some reason fall out and he would be called upon to play the leading role.

I may be prejudiced, but I have to acknowledge that Imelda would have been a pretty catch for any young chap with a drop of good red blood in his veins. The delicacy of her person and her purity of feature and form were matched by her tender heart, her wonderful natural sympathy for all living and suffering things, her instinctive understanding of the needs and desires of those she loved. Yet there was also a strangeness about her, something wild and foreign and unfathomable, and a wilfulness too, a surprising determination in the last analysis to make her own decisions and go her own way. It was to this element in her personality that I feared that Frank might, in some perverse way, appeal.

As Hubert approached manhood, he came rapidly to intellectual maturity. Previously very much an outdoor character, a fine sportsman who had hoped at one time to make a career in the Royal Air Force, he acquired towards the end of his distinguished school career a wide range of scholarly interests, and chose to pursue these at St Andrews University. By this date he was tallish, sturdily built, slow in speech but deeply thoughtful, never expressing an opinion until it had been properly considered and found to be adequate. His strong Scottish face was surmounted by a fine head of springy, reddish-auburn hair, and his grey-blue eyes were kindly and steady. He always reminded me strongly of Gordon Jackson, the well-known actor. He had already made a profound study of philosophy, and while still an undergraduate was considered a leading authority on Leibnitz. From adolescence he had been plagued by digestive problems, an affliction which he bore with courage, uncomplaining patience and a wry, self-deprecating humour. His deep affection for Imelda was most touching to observe: he treated her with wonderful consideration, was sensitive to her every little worry and need, and at all times showed her a lovely old-fashioned courtesy and deference. With Frank he was patient and long-suffering far beyond the call of duty.

His brother, by contrast, grew up a brittle and effeminate fop.

His self-satisfaction was utterly inordinate, and in reality there was remarkably little to justify it in terms either of personal attributes or solid achievements. He made himself out a tremendous ladies' man, but I harboured strong suspicions that he had formed a homosexual relationship with one of the estate workers with whom he was always hanging about. He considered himself a great intellectual, and was always attempting to trip Hubert up or catch him out in abstract discussion, but his arguments were uniformly glib, facile, shallow and meretricious. In gentle mockery of his overweening conceit, Imelda had christened him 'Superbo', but the inflated youth chose to interpret the slight as a compliment, and readily accepted the cutting designation. In person he was slight and insignificant, with a sallow complexion and rather girlish features; his voice was querulous and epicene. He was altogether a person whom it was an effort to tolerate and quite impossible to warm to.

When Superbo left school, by which time Hubert had completed his first year at St Andrews, he settled down at Lemington and steadfastly refused either to go to university or to undertake any gainful employment whatsoever. He had done not badly at school and with a little discipline could, I suppose, have made a student, but he much preferred to remain at home in idleness, sniffing around Imelda's skirts. He was like one of those spoken of by St Paul in his Second Epistle to the Thessalonians: "For we hear that there are some who walk among you disorderly, working not at all, but are busybodies." Had the matter been in my hands I would have applied the Apostle's solution: "If any would not work, neither should he eat." Unfortunately there were limits to my authority in the matter, which it would have been highly improper in me to have overstepped. The boy's natural father was alive and well, after all, but in this as in so many other things he was wholly impotent and irresolute. Frank represented himself to his parents as being actively engaged in research on mycology, that is the scientific study of mushrooms and other fungi. So far as I could ascertain, however, his knowledge of the subject never extended much beyond what he could have gleaned from *The Observer's Book of Toadstools* or some publication of that nature. He was a typical example of the class of person who used to be dignified by the name of 'dreamer', but who is in reality nothing other than bone idle.

As time passed I became increasingly concerned about the complicating and disruptive influence which Superbo introduced into the otherwise straightforward, and potentially idyllic, relationship between Imelda and Hubert. There was little serious doubt that Imelda's commitment to the latter was real and deep, and that with every passing month she was more irresistibly attracted to the fine young man. As to Hubert, there was never any question in his mind that Imelda would some day be his bride, the cherished partner of his life's joys, sorrows and achievements, and ultimately the mistress of Lemington. Equally clear, however, was Superbo's envious ambition to supplant him. Often I found myself suspecting that his longings for Imelda were a less powerful determinant of his conduct than his bitter urge to defeat and humiliate the elder brother in whose shadow he languished, and to whose status of firstborn were added superiority in every natural endowment and a clear supremacy in human excellence. However that might be, Frank had certainly persuaded *himself* that he was in love, and it was a constant source of worry to me that Imelda might quite inadvertently encourage, or at least might fail adequately to discourage, the amorous ambitions of the infatuated stripling.

It is relevant here to stress Imelda's natural kindliness of disposition, her reluctance to hurt so much as a fly, far less a human being, and her readiness always to put the most generous possible interpretation on human motives. Even as a child she had been at pains not to let Frank feel too *left out* in a situation in which he was inescapably the superfluous third attaching himself to a pair inherently self-sufficient; and it is entirely possible that his vanity had led him to put on this admirable sensitivity of conduct a quite false construction. Imelda had been brought up from the cradle with the acutest consciousness of the difference between right and wrong, and had she seen the true tendency of Superbo's emotions, it is unquestionable that she would have recoiled in horror from the advances of the arrogant and envious wretch. But she was far too trusting, and too pure in her own feelings, to be quick to suspect infamy in others.

There is another aspect of the matter which needs to be addressed here, a truth about the female nature which it would be dishonest to shirk. A certain degree of natural flirtatiousness is an invariable and indeed a charming facet of the feminine character. It means, of course, precisely nothing in relation to the deep and constant feelings of such a woman as Imelda; but that is not always the way things may appear to the recipient of such passing favours. Superbo was predisposed both by vanity and by wishful thinking to suppose Imelda's gentle and evanescent dalliance the mark of what he wanted it to be—true love. For her part, secure in the love of her precious Hubert, she may well have taken a little innocent pleasure in knowing that she possessed the power to attract a rival, and to introduce in that way a certain element of piquancy—a playful little challenge to her intended, perhaps—into a relationship which was so perfect that it might otherwise almost have been in danger of becoming a trifle boring.

All this would doubtless have been harmless enough had it not been for the traces of mental instability which I had detected in Frank even when he was a child, and which, with his assumption of the character of 'Superbo', threatened to become much more pronounced and infinitely more dangerous. The unpredictability of behaviour to which this warp of nature might lead put an entirely new and a perilous complexion on his preoccupation with Imelda, for whose happiness and well-being I was of course responsible. Whether it was truly a mental illness or at bottom a disease of the *soul*, I am not equipped to pass judgement.

Originally manifesting itself generally in an outrageous inflation and an almost paranoid jealousy of poor Hubert—who felt nothing but affection and pity for his morally crippled younger brother—the affliction began gradually to demonstrate a more specific symptomatology. The first odd symptom which I noted was a quite irrational and evil disposition towards old Flight Sergeant, the family bulldog. Flight Sergeant was deeply loved by everyone else in the household, and always regarded as really Hubert's pet; Hubert had named him and raised him as his own, and whenever he was at home the old dog waddled faithfully and affectionately behind him wherever he went. It is my belief that the antagonism which Superbo manifested towards old Flight

Sergeant was really a displaced expression of his resentment towards Hubert: by persecuting the animal he 'got at' his brother and gave rein to a hostility which he was too cowardly to express directly.

I recall one occasion with particular vividness. One beautiful summer evening Imelda, Hubert and Frank decided to go for a stroll in the Lemington woods. I remember Imelda remarking jokingly that if, on such a romantic evening—and here she flashed a smile of delightful conspiracy at her beloved Hubert—they failed to hear a nightingale, she would be unassuageably disappointed. They set off, accompanied by the old bulldog. About half an hour later I was in the gun-room when old Flight Sergeant came limping in, dishevelled and whining pitifully. I was astonished, and not a little worried, by his obvious distress, though I did not see how the trio could possibly have come to any harm. Inquiring later of Imelda, I was told in shocked tones that Superbo had kicked the poor old creature most viciously, merely because he had disturbed the peace of the evening by making a small noise that was quite natural and, in an animal well past his prime and not in the best of health, readily to be excused. It had cost Imelda all her charms to calm the normally placid Hubert, and to restrain him from striking the unnatural wretch.

An even more dreadful and inexcusable incident took place about six months later. The progress of old Flight Sergeant's internal ailment had gradually rendered his vicinity intolerable even to those who loved him most; and finding him one day whining pitifully and in great pain, I took it upon myself, in Hubert's absence, to summon the veterinary surgeon from Duns to have him put to sleep. It was a necessary decision, but a hard one. The following day I devised what I think almost all of those present agreed was a touching little ceremony to say farewell to the faithful old creature. In tender arms the fine old soul was borne to his last resting-place by the ha-ha; as the poet lamented:

O! fine old Soul! In hodden grey
We mourn thy Passing on a Summer's Day.

The season was actually winter, but the sentiment is unaffected. I spoke a few carefully chosen words over the grave; and it was then, at the most solemn moment, as the earth was being replaced, that Superbo, who had been hanging around at some distance looking disaffected from the proceedings, outraged everyone present by delivering a Fascist salute. This was for some reason pointed unmistakably in my own direction. Superbo followed up this act of unparalleled insolence and effrontery by bursting into a fit of hysterical laughter which I judged–correctly, as later events were to prove–to be actually insane. Finally he rounded off the unseemly display by dashing precipitately away into the house. The ineffaceable impression which I received from this exhibition was that, by taking such unholy glee in old Flight Sergeant's otherwise universally regretted demise, Superbo was doing nothing less than wishing death upon the brother with whom the dog was so closely identified.

By this date, I think, Hubert and Imelda had announced their engagement. That event, had I but known it, represented the peak of my happiness at Lemington, as I rejoiced in the promise that all my hopes would soon be realised and the nagging worries occasioned by Superbo and his unconscionable behaviour put behind me at last. Little did I guess that from then on our affairs would be in sad declension, that our fond prospects were destined all too soon to be blighted by tragedy and disaster. At first I believed that Superbo had inwardly accepted defeat, and I awaited with confidence the day when he would have swallowed his pride sufficiently to take himself off from among us and start making a life of his own elsewhere. It was not to be. Month after month the stubborn mushroom-gazer continued to mooch about the estate in disgraceful idleness, and I was soon to learn that his ignoble intentions towards his brother's bride-to-be had been in no way abandoned.

The only distinctly visible cloud on the horizon at the time of the engagement had been the state of Hubert's health. His digestive problem, now diagnosed as a duodenal ulcer, fluctuated in intensity and was always exacerbated by spells of particularly hard study and by the proximity of examinations, which the academically highly conscientious young man always took with commendable seriousness. At Christmas time that year his condition was particularly bad, and he had to retire early after

Christmas Dinner in considerable pain. Superbo had been in an aggressive and offensive mood all evening, and left the table in a huff after the port had gone round. Such behaviour at the season of good will was extremely upsetting to his parents, and I decided to go out to the terrace–where I suspected he had retreated to sulk–in order to remonstrate with him and if possible persuade him to come back in and rejoin the party. Conceive of my horror when, on opening the French windows, I surprised the epicene stripling wantonly forcing his attentions on his brother's fiancée, and my ward.

I say 'forcing his attentions', and I dare say that was the way it started, but the embrace did appear to be what I believe is called a 'passionate' one, and I am forced to admit that there must on this occasion have been at least a degree of complicity on the part of Imelda. Let us say that she was carried away by the Christmas spirit and by the not ungenerous samplings of the riches of the Lemington cellars which we had all of us enjoyed. No such excuse could properly be made for Superbo, who for years now had been cynically bent on her desecration. I do not think that I have ever been more hardly put to restrain myself from striking a man in the presence of a woman; but Superbo's wretched physique would in any case have rendered such a course of action dishonourable. Containing my fury with difficulty, I escorted Imelda out of his presence and ordered her to bed. Then I went into urgent consultation with the parents of the infatuated youth.

Fortunately, my brother-in-law displayed on this occasion a firmness that was very far from being characteristic of him: I conclude that his religious sensibilities had been outraged by what had occurred. He was entirely in agreement with me that Frank could not be allowed to remain any longer at Lemington unless he was prepared to work for his living. Privately, I have to admit, I hoped that his distaste for industry would be sufficient to insure his speedy departure. In any case, it was essential that he and Imelda be absolutely forbidden ever to be alone together. These basic points readily agreed upon by Charles and myself, I suggested that a family conference be held immediately after Hubert's return to St Andrews in order to have the whole business frankly aired and thoroughly thrashed out. It was, of course, essential that

Hubert be kept in entire ignorance of what had occurred. His medical condition was one which is always greatly worsened, if not actually precipitated, by stress, tension or worry, and to divulge even a hint of the trouble that had arisen could have the most serious consequences.

Imelda was deeply ashamed of her fleeting fall from grace, and begged for nothing else than that it should be utterly forgotten by everyone and that she should be allowed to make up for the lapse by devoting herself, even more unstintingly than before, to the needs and the love of the splendid man whom she had thoughtlessly but not maliciously wronged. She said as much at the family conference, quite openly and of her own accord, and her repentance was readily accepted and the opportunity for rehabilitation granted. My sister was of the view that sheer boredom was at the bottom of it all, and that Imelda would benefit greatly from spending the time before her marriage at an excellent Swiss finishing school which she had heard about. I own that I was of her opinion; but Imelda pleaded so eloquently and so movingly against being parted from Hubert that my resolution was broken and it was agreed that she should remain at Lemington.

In the case of Superbo no mitigation was possible and no compromise offered. Either he could remain at Lemington and do an honest day's work on the estate, or he could leave. He chose to remain. In order that justice might be seen to be done, it was necessary that some token penalty be exacted from Imelda, and it was decided that she should be prepared to help about the house a bit as might be needed. This requirement was never more than a formality, however, and was never strictly insisted upon. Imelda had always, as it happened, been more than a willing helper. For Superbo, serious forestry work was decided upon. I was sure that he would not last a week, but I must acknowledge that I was wrong. Though utterly unfitted for such labour by habit and physique, he persisted doggedly in a way which had far more in it of spitefulness than of courage. He was so physically useless as to be little more than a burden to his fellow workers, but took a malicious pride in not giving up; bathed in sweat and sometimes nearly dropping from exhaustion, he fumbled on until lowsing-time day after day and week after week, just in order to have the

sweet satisfaction of scoring a point off his old Uncle Affleck. One
could not altogether withhold a measure of admiration, but it was
an admiration that clear-sightedly recognised the fundamental
perversity of its object.

This régime continued until the final return of Hubert from St
Andrews at mid-summer. The return was a triumphant one. Four
years of unremittingly diligent study, combined with exceptional
innate gifts as a metaphysician, had been recognised by the award
of first class honours in Philosophy. Hubert had been accepted,
moreover, to read for his Bachelor of Philosophy degree at
Oxford the following year prior to seeking a professional appointment, and in October he would go into residence at my old
college, Lincoln. The day of his 'capping' was the proudest of his
life. There to see him graduate was his beautiful and adored
Imelda, and though I was not myself present on the occasion I can
well imagine the humble pride, if I may be permitted a justifiable
oxymoron, with which he must have shown her off to his friends
and companions. The future, that wonderful afternoon in early
July, must have seemed fair indeed. But Fortune is a fickle
mistress and those who worship her build their houses upon the
sand. How could Hubert, or any of those who loved him, have
guessed that less than half a year of life was left to him?

For much of that summer a remarkable appearance of harmony
was observable among the perennial threesome of Hubert, Imelda
and Superbo. Imelda's pride in Hubert, and her joy at having him
back with her at Lemington, were touching to behold. I had high
hopes that Superbo had been chastened by his recent experience,
and that he was now preparing himself to accept the coming
marriage with as much grace as he was capable of mustering. The
nuptials had been postponed, in fact, until the following summer
because of Hubert's coming year at Oxford: it would not be
possible for him to get the most out of college life if he were
already in the married state. This was to be no more than a joy
deferred, however. But the contentment and the deceptive
harmony of those brief months were soon to prove the lull before
the storm.

As the summer wore on into early autumn a strange sadness
seemed to settle on Hubert. Perhaps the expected parting from

Imelda was enough to account for it, though this was no worse than they had grown accustomed to in the St Andrews years. True, he would be geographically more distant on this occasion, but that alone could not have been expected to produce such a marked change of mood. As the weeks passed the recently so buoyant and contented young man appeared to sink into a spirit-less depression. I was determined to get to the bottom of the matter and questioned him closely about his feelings, but he insisted that all was well and attributed the decline of his spirits to a slight recurrence of his gastric condition. I was unable to extract from him even a hint of any deeper cause.

With a heavy heart I was forced to admit into consciousness the message of the nagging voice—which at first I attempted to disregard—which told me that that snake Superbo had once more bound the happiness of the betrothed pair within his envious coils. He himself was impossible to fathom—he was as expert at concealing his feelings as he was at covering his tracks. But Imelda was far from being such a closed book to the old uncle who had lovingly cared for her and been minutely attentive to her every need, physical and spiritual, ever since she had come to him as a helpless eight year-old orphan. That September I observed how she fluctuated from wild, almost manic excitement to states of deep unhappiness much more dramatic than Hubert's, when she shed tears freely and gave every appearance of baffled frustration, but resolutely refused to tell me what the matter was. Though kept in ignorance of the exact nature of the trouble I had my own natural and very strong suspicions, which I only much later had the opportunity to discover might have been, on this occasion, quite wide of the mark. Suspecting what I did, I knew that it was my duty to act, and the course of action I took was based on the supposition that Superbo was once more intent upon upsetting the lovely apple-cart of mutual love.

What I decided upon was that Imelda must go south with Hubert, not as his wife and most certainly not (need I say?) as his mistress, but to live separately somewhere in his vicinity while he pursued his avocations at Oxford. By good fortune, my sister had dear and long-standing friends who lived in the Oxfordshire village of Charlton-on-Otmoor, and this childless couple proved to be more than delighted that Imelda should be their guest for as long as might turn out to be necessary. Imelda received the decision meekly and compliantly, without any great appearance of either joy or sorrow, and thereafter seemed more settled, though scarcely ebullient. What surprised me most was Hubert's reaction, his listless lack of enthusiasm. While not objecting to the scheme in any way and indeed professing himself happy with it, he gave no sign at all of coming out of his depression.

I was greatly saddened at this time by a change in his attitude to myself, the appearance of a certain distance and coldness, as if he were disappointed in me, almost as if he had discovered something to my discredit which he lacked the stomach to broach with me. I own I was completely baffled. What perhaps came to torment me most was the suspicion which grew upon me that Superbo might have been telling his brother lies about me, calumnies which anyone who really knew me must reject at once as preposterous, but which might, all the same, have been enough to disturb, by their very effrontery, Hubert's fundamentally trusting nature, and make him long for a reassurance which he would have thought it quite shameful to demand of me. Let me then say here and now, once and for all—and leave it at that—that my love for Imelda, and my devotion to her, were always solely those of a father, a father by choice who knew all the tenderness—and more—which any natural father would have felt for his fleshly issue. It is humiliating to be obliged to make such a declaration, and I resent the necessity, but both self-respect and respect for the truth make the duty unavoidable. I shall not refer to this matter again.

My plan was put into operation, Hubert and Imelda departed for the south at the beginning of October and for the better part of two months an ominous calm reigned at Lemington. I kept a close watch on Superbo, and not without reason, for at this time he began displaying even odder behavioural patterns than heretofore, signs which heralded his not long delayed collapse into irreclaimable madness. He disappeared for hours at a time on long, lone walks, and as he wandered about the estate it was observed that he not only talked to himself frequently, often shouting and gesticulating, but sometimes appeared to be engaged in dialogue with invisible others. Occasionally he could be seen gazing up into the sky as if mesmerised, waiting, it would appear, for divine guidance. He also took to spending long periods locked up in his room listening to Germanic music, particularly Wagner. In contrast to his loquaciousness when alone, he was uniformly sullen and taciturn in company, so that meal times, when he was present, (he frequently absented himself), took on something of a purgatorial quality. I advised his parents to seek medical advice, but his mother was already so taken up with wedding preparations that she scarcely listened, while Charles merely nodded vaguely and looked worried, which was perhaps the nearest approach to taking action of which he was capable.

During all these weeks a postcard or two was all the news we had of the pair at Oxford. In the last week of November, however, a phone call was received from Hubert which for one of his normally equable and philosophical disposition could almost be described as frantic. Imelda's physical and mental health had broken down alarmingly, he claimed, and she was determined to come home to consult Dr Downie, our trusted and longstanding family physician. Being more than anxious to keep her away from Superbo in both of their present states of mind, I argued strongly for her being treated at Oxford, but Hubert was adamant. Apart from other considerations, he told me, there had been a recurrence of her enuresis, and her continuing to stay at Charlton-on-Otmoor would therefore at the moment be something of an imposition on her kind hosts. What could one say? Hubert's own gastric ailment had deteriorated drastically as a result of all this worry, but he was determined not to interrupt his studies; he had made an appointment to consult a specialist in Oxford, and he intended, after bringing Imelda to Lemington and staying the weekend, to return there to keep it.

I come now to the heaviest, the most painful and the most poignant part of my tale. Pausing to recruit my dwindling reserves of strength, and realising my reluctance to embark upon this dreadful part of the narrative, I am aware of how much the composition of this memoir has already cost me. I am close to exhaustion; my heart is palpitating and thumping irregularly, my eyelids are twitching and my eyes themselves burning and smarting, while my old skin seems utterly to have lost its last traces of resilience, so that when I knit my brow and then relax the muscles, it feels to me almost as if the skin stays where it was, knitted. I am almost dropping with tiredness: but the weariness of the old body is but a pale reflection of the weariness of the spirit. Everyone I have loved has gone before me, and Lemington is now a kind of glorified guest house . . . But I am becoming an old bore. Duty calls, and I cannot evade the chronicling of the time when all my fondest hopes and dreams were erased for ever.

The dear young people arrived home on the Friday evening, and I was shocked at the condition of both of them. Hubert looked drawn, strained, and utterly exhausted. Imelda, though pale, was much less ill-looking physically than I had feared, but she seemed in the grip of an extraordinary kind of suppressed agitation. Even with me she was quite unforthcoming about her symptoms, insisting that she wanted to see Dr Downie before talking about her illness to anyone else. It was one of those occasions when she exhibited that thrawnness that was a genuine element in her nature, but which she only called up as a defence when her circumstances were particularly distressing. Over the weekend she remained almost all the time in her bedroom, and had her meals brought up on a tray. I was glad enough about this, because it kept her away from the prying eyes of Superbo, who was noticed on more than one occasion indulging in what I can only call spying.

That weekend was a tense one for all of us, and in spite of all our efforts Hubert never succeeded in relaxing even a little until the Sunday evening. He was due to leave for Oxford the following morning, and I think, frankly, that he was glad to be going. He managed to smile and even joke a little at dinner, and I remember him commenting favourably on cook's venison casserole. Perhaps he should not have eaten it; it may have been too rich. I bade him goodnight at about eleven o'clock and he said that he would be going up himself very shortly. He was not unfriendly but the old warmth was not there. I never saw him conscious again.

Some time in the small hours of the morning–I cannot recall

exactly when–I was aroused by a timid yet at the same time urgent knocking on my door. Being a light sleeper I was awake at once and lost no time in opening to my brother-in-law, who was in a state of quite unbelievable agitation. He was scarcely coherent, but I understood that Hubert had been found unconscious on the floor of his bedroom. When I got there I helped his parents and brother to lay him on the bed; seeing him stretched there, barely breathing and ghastly in his pallor, I knew instinctively and at once there he was already beyond help. However on the insistence of his mother I attempted artificial respiration, but to no avail. Superbo, it appeared, had heard sounds of distress, and going out to the corridor had encountered poor Hubert doubled up in agony, lathered in sweat and looking already like a ghost, but still attempting to go for help. With commendable alacrity Frank had rushed off at once to ring for the doctor rather than waste time in giving assistance; when he returned with his parents, whom he had awakened, Hubert was lying face down on the floor of his bedroom. He had previously been vomiting, it appeared, with appalling violence. Three adults were not enough to lift him and it was then that Charles had awakened me.

During the few minutes between my arrival on the scene and that of Dr Downie, the full extent of the catastrophe was borne in on me. Everything was in ruins: my splendid young nephew almost certainly gone, his life of burgeoning promise cut off while scarcely out of the bud; my poor little Imelda a widow, as it were, before she could be a bride; all my hopes for the future of the family dashed to pieces; the mad and grotesque Superbo now heir to Lemington. Knowing all this, sure in myself that the disaster was irreversible, shocked by the suddenness of a grief to which I cannot begin to give expression, I still had to find within me the strength to hold the family together, to be a rock of support to the crumbling parents, to be ready to give such little comfort as was possible to my bereaved ward when she should learn of this horror.

When Dr Downie arrived he at once ordered an ambulance, but I think we all realised that it was too late: all vital signs were now absent. I assumed that Hubert's ulcer had perforated, and this proved to be correct. It is probable that he died of shock, but he must have been in great pain for several hours: no doubt it was his characteristic selflessness and consideration for others which stayed him from seeking help earlier, but it is a tragic irony that this virtue may well have proved fatal. There was no dubiety about the cause of death, none at all. It was peritonitis resulting from a perforated duodenal ulcer. Dr Downie signed the death certificate. He can be trusted implicitly; I have known him almost all my life and he was in the form below me at Uppingham.

With what, objectively speaking, must be termed utter irresponsibility, Superbo had, after phoning for the ambulance, woken Imelda and brought her down to witness the death agony of her beloved. In his defence I ought in justice to say that he was himself in such an hysterical frame of mind that he was probably incapable of thinking through the consequences of his actions. Imelda fainted away almost immediately upon laying eyes on the prostrated Hubert, and for a week or more she remained in an extremely dangerous condition. She was, of course, unable to attend the funeral service, which was conducted by a pompous Episcopalian priest named Father Goodlad, some acquaintance of Charles's I believe. He exhibited in full measure that irritating propensity of clerics at funerals, to dilate upon the virtues of the deceased at great length as if they had known them intimately, when in fact they probably knew nothing about them at all until a few minutes previously. I must confess that I felt Father Goodlad as an intrusive presence, but Charles would have been quite incapable of conducting the service, though he did try to assist. As it was he broke down pitifully the first time he attempted to say a prayer. To my brother-in-law's weakness of character, and his inadequacy as both husband and father, may ultimately be traced, I believe, most of the ills which afflicted the family at Lemington in those tragic years.

Hubert was gone and he could never be brought back. All my care was now for my poor Imelda, who must slowly be nursed back to health and helped to start life anew amidst the ruins of all her hopes and dreams. Her grief was heart-rending, and at first I was not privy to the poignant circumstance which by a cruel yet tender paradox at once heightened and assuaged it. But one morning, seeming stronger and more composed than she had been since before Hubert's death, though still very pale and weak, she took my hand, breathed deeply as if to steady her nerves, and told me that there was something she wanted me to know before Dr Downie found it out, which he must assuredly do very soon. Imelda was with child. Some time during the late summer she and Hubert had yielded to the overwhelming pressure of their feelings—as I understood it, on more than one occasion. This was the result. Imelda laid her hand upon her womb, looked up at me with a weary yet radiant smile, and said quietly, 'A little of Hubert is still with us, you see.'

My heart was a riot of conflicting emotions. Under normal circumstances the shame which would be brought on the family, and my disappointment in the two young people whom I so loved and whom I had trusted implicitly, would perhaps have predominated. But now I could not feel the least anger towards my poor girl or my late unhappy nephew. I shared for Imelda's sake in the sense of comfort which the forthcoming event brought to her, and I was myself a little comforted by the thought that Hubert was to leave behind him some living legacy. At the same time, I was more acutely aware than Imelda was, I think, of the formidable difficulties of her situation. But at least I now understood the cause of Hubert's strange dejection at the end of the summer and of his changed attitude to myself. For all his metaphysics, the straight and honest young chap was a good and sincere Christian, and his fall from grace must have occasioned acute feelings of guilt, and, in relation to myself, self-castigation, because he had let me down and broken the complete trust which I had always placed in him. How I would have reacted had he still been alive I do not know, but now I could feel nothing but pity for the situation in which he had found himself, and sorrow that the shadow of an event of which I had been wholly ignorant had come between us at the last.

I saw, too, how foolish I had been to imagine that Superbo could ever have effected a rupture between those committed lovers. I had quite misinterpreted the signs of that summer. I almost began to feel sorry for my misjudgement of Superbo, until I called to mind that in respect of his *intentions* it was no misjudgement at all; if he could have prised Hubert and Imelda apart he would have done so, and his failure was no credit to his moral fibre but rather a reflection of his incapacity. With that thought, however, came a warning intimation that the situation was now utterly changed. Hubert was gone and Imelda was in an intensely vulnerable position. What might have been unthinkable three months ago seemed now like an all too probable outcome. Lost and griefstricken and in need of a father for her child, Imelda might well, in a moment of rashness, of precipitate folly, throw herself into the arms of the only other man whom she had ever known in the least intimately, with whom all her past associations were inextricably mingled. I saw that it was a matter of the utmost urgency that Imelda should be kept away from Superbo during the months of her pregnancy.

Under the pressure of these considerations my mind was now racing. Another potential complication at once presented itself. It was unavoidably necessary to involve Hubert's parents in the decisions which must now be taken: but Hubert's parents were also the parents of Superbo. True, they were painfully disappointed in him and deeply disapproving of his way of life, but they could not be expected to take quite such an objective view of him as that of which I was capable. To me it was clear that he was mentally unbalanced and potentially dangerous, an utterly unthinkable partner for my tender Imelda. To them, however, he was their only surviving child, and the heir to Lemington, and with Hubert's death it was entirely natural that they should cleave to him with renewed affection, however meagre his deserts. What more comforting prospect for the grieving pair than that their surviving son should become the father of their grandchild, the spouse of their daughter-in-law elect? As I thought of all this I envisaged ranged against me a united front of my sister and Charles, Imelda and Superbo, a combination which even I, with my considerable knowledge and experience of human nature, could not be confident of withstanding. I must act at once to forestall such a possibility.

I had one great advantage: I was certainly aware of all this long before it could possibly have entered the minds of the old couple. So far, they did not even know of the pregnancy—nor indeed did Superbo. As soon as he did, it was certain that he would seek to take every possible advantage of the situation. He was utterly unscrupulous and possessed of a certain crafty, scheming intelligence. I must therefore persuade Charles and my sister to my point of view before he could set to work on Imelda. It was essential, first of all, that he should not have access to her, and since she was still weak enough to warrant being confined to her room this was not a great difficulty. As a precaution, I insisted that on no account should she open the door to him, and she readily agreed. It would not be possible to keep the coming event a secret from Superbo, and I felt therefore that it would be best if the necessary discussion were carried out in his presence, so that any moves he might make could be noted and countered as necessary.

I made the announcement to the gathered family at lunch time, therefore, and allowed the initial tearful emotions to be unleashed and the first flustered thoughts expressed without too much interference or directiveness on my part. To my surprise, and I confess slightly to my alarm, Superbo took the news with poker-face imperturbability and made no contribution to the discussion. I had been expecting something different, and his lack of reaction put me more alertly on guard rather than otherwise. The predominant emotion which emerged was happiness, even joy, on the part of the prospective grandparents that their deeply mourned son would now leave offspring for their comfort and delight. For my own part, I was by no means convinced that it was in Imelda's ultimate interests that she should keep the child. Without it, she could start life afresh wherever she chose and put her sorrow behind her for ever. With it, she would in all probability be tied to Lemington and its familial support, and at the same time remain in pressing need of a husband: the combination of these two factors pointed ominously towards the ascendancy and the ultimate triumph of Superbo. To argue strongly in favour of adoption at this stage (abortion was out of the question in this Christian household) might well be counter-productive: it was Imelda on whom this course of action must be urged, for it was easy to argue to the others that her own wishes in the matter must be respected. The birth was still six months distant; what was now of pressing urgency was that she should be removed from Lemington at least until it had taken place.

That afternoon I went over the whole matter with Imelda quite calmly and dispassionately—without, of course, allowing Frank's name to enter into the discussion even for an instant. The points I made to her were the same as those I later put to my sister and brother-in-law: the unpleasantness of having her subjected to local gossip in the months to come, the damaging effect this would have on the family and its honour, above all the need for her to be in an environment that was not loaded at every point with memories and associations which at the present time and in her present condition could only cause pain and sadness.

At first Imelda pled with tears to be allowed to remain at home at Lemington, but though treating her with all kindness and consideration I was firm and unyielding on this point. In her weakened state of health, exhausted and worn down by grief, she acquiesced without further struggle. It was agreed that she should return to her kind friends at Charlton-on-Otmoor until after the birth. This point gained, I thought it well to strike while the iron was hot, and gently insinuated the idea of adoption. I did not urge it strongly, merely planting a seed which could be left to grow, and later nurtured as appropriate. Imelda did not say much in response to this suggestion, but her air of quiet sadness somehow indicated to me that this battle, too, would finally be won.

The argument in favour of Charlton-on-Otmoor was readily carried—that is, my sister was persuaded to accept it without undue difficulty. Charles's views, in so far as he had any, frankly no longer counted. Superbo, on hearing the decision, dashed out of the room in a frenzy. I knew what he was about to attempt, and I knew that he would be unsuccessful, so I let him go. Any delay, however, could only work in his favour. A long telephone call to the accommodating friends in Oxfordshire, explaining the case in its broad outlines and gratefully begging their further help and co-operation, proved entirely satisfactory in its results. Within a couple of days I set off for Charlton-on-Otmoor with Imelda. I stayed the weekend and saw her settled in, then left her in the firm confidence that she was in caring and loving hands.

On my return to Lemington I learned that Superbo had accepted defeat at last, and departed. It may be that my fears about his intentions would in the end have proved groundless, for I believe now that Imelda's pregnancy had in all likelihood delivered a fatal blow to his pride. Hubert had triumphed over him in death in a way that could never be gainsaid or denied. No doubt it was this humiliation which precipitated the final loss of his reason. Superbo went, I understand, to Edinburgh, where within two or three months he collapsed into lurid insanity, a raging madman overwhelmed by paranoid delusions. The effectual loss of their second son, coming so hard on the heels of their awful bereavement, broke the remaining spirit and health of the poor parents, and within four years of this date both of them were in the grave.

In mid-June of the following year Imelda was delivered in Oxford of a healthy girl. She wrote to me announcing the event and informed me, without comment, that she had decided on adoption. One curious stipulation she made, and she made it with an insistence that seemed to say that it would brook no denial. I knew from of old this streak of stubborn self-will in Imelda, and I decided not to resist it overtly. She wished her child to be adopted in Berwickshire and brought up as close as possible to Lemington, and she asked me to make arrangements for this to be done. She herself would live in England, but she would come north to hand the baby over to its adoptive parents. I made haste to give effect to her wishes.

As it happened, there was an excellent childless couple living in one of the estate cottages whom I knew to be considering adoption. I knew both husband and wife to be absolutely trustworthy and discreet, and in order to pre-empt their natural curiosity and obviate the need for speculation I decided to make a clean breast of the true circumstances. While I had full confidence that Imelda's child would be going to a good home, I thought it highly undesirable from every point of view that she should be brought up on the Lemington estate. Such a situation would have been intolerably painful for the grandparents, who were extremely distressed at Imelda's decision, and in the course of time could not have failed to be a source of all kinds of gossip and tittle-tattle in the neighbourhood which would have lowered the family's reputation and good name quite intolerably. I therefore concealed the transaction from Charles and my sister, a move of which Imelda readily saw the sense, and made out that the baby had been found a home in Edinburgh. My further step I naturally kept from Imelda. The adoptive father, Dan Johnstone, who worked for us as a tractorman, had, I knew, been considering leaving agricultural employment to seek work in the industrial lowlands, and I quietly made it readily possible for him to do so without financial anxiety. The little family left the district when the baby was about six months old.

The tears which Imelda must have cried had, I think, already been shed when she arrived at Lemington with her bonny and happy bairn. Throughout the few days she remained she was cool and collected and business-like. The heartbroken grandparents had been persuaded to take a short holiday in Strathspey, so she and I were alone together. This is the hardest part of all my story to tell, and if I were not writing it as much for myself as for any future reader I would probably flinch from it. My Imelda treated me throughout her visit with the utmost coldness and detachment. She gave the appearance of conversing with me only with the greatest reluctance, and when she did so it was only on the most indifferent topics. I knew that she blamed me for the loss of her child, but what could I do about it now?

On the morning the baby was to be handed over I accompanied her to the farm cottage. Imelda explained all the baby's little needs and preferences to her new mother, unpacked her linen and had a look round. Seeming satisfied, she wished the parents good luck and shook their hands; then she kissed the baby on the top of her head and walked out of the door. I watched her walk slowly off through the woods in the direction of the dell. "I shall see you at lunch!" I cried after her, but she did not reply. In a state of some agitation, I myself strode off up the drive to get some exercise and master my feelings. When I returned to the house Imelda's little blue Mini was gone and her room was empty. I never saw her or received any communication from her again.

I am an old, sick, weary man. Perhaps I am also a wicked one; but I ask any kind person who may read this memoir not to judge me too harshly. If I have caused suffering to others I have suffered equally in my turn. Everything I did, I did for the good of something whose interests transcend those of any individual: the family. The family of which I wrote is now no more, so there is nothing more for me to say. I am tired, and it is time for me to slip off to rest.

Fingleton Den Cottage,
Lemington, Berwickshire

6 May 1986

Dear Mrs Moodie,

After sending you the photocopies and photographs last week I sat down and re-read the originals, and immediately began to regret that I had not made a number of further points to you before posting the material. It had been some time, in fact, since I had looked at either of the memoirs, and I failed perhaps to appreciate how some of the content might disturb you.

The first point I want to make, then, is that I am quite certain that Superbo (under which designation I can't now help thinking of Frank) is *not* your father. As you will have realised, he is essentially a fantasist, totally immersed in sick delusions concerning his supposed former romantic relations with your mother, and everything that he writes has to be taken with a very large pinch of salt, to say the least. I am sure you appreciate this yourself; but still, even the least ghost of a possibility that you could be the child of a paranoid schizophrenic—victim of a malady which, as you will know, may often carry a hereditary component—could not fail to be upsetting, especially at a time when you are yourself carrying a child. Rest assured, then, that Superbo is quite deluded. I am personally convinced that the excellent Hubert was indeed your father: a man whose portrait as painted by his envious brother is a loathsome parody; a man who, had he lived, might now stand in the front rank of contemporary philosophers.

On the other hand, I should perhaps caution you against identifying the truth *too* closely with Uncle Affleck's account of the events of your parents' youth. Uncle Affleck was a sterling old fellow, but for some reason he had from the very start—i.e. from the time when he first arrived at Lemington—a marked and irrational aversion to poor Superbo, which the weak character and unstable mentality of your uncle could only partially justify. You will have noted that Frank himself was in spite of everything an unstinting admirer of Uncle Affleck, and seems never to have suspected just how little his regard was reciprocated. One other small point I might just mention, and leave it at that: Uncle Affleck's nickname at Uppingham was, I believe, 'Mendax'.

Sir Robert could not, of course, bring himself to recount the fate of your mother during the years which followed the tragedy which overtook her with the death of Hubert. He seems to have blamed himself quite unjustly for what happened (I mean, for her having become pregnant to your father long before their planned marriage). Why, I will never know. Certain remarks he made to me in his last years I could only interpret in that way. His sense of responsibility for Imelda, and his devotion to her, appear to have been almost excessive, and the strength of his emotions must have exacerbated his tender conscience in this regard.

At any rate, you are certain to ask what became of your unhappy mother, and I am duty bound to tell you. As I explained before, though, I know very little about it all. Imelda went to London in 1964 and led a gay and irresponsible and, according to some, a disgraceful and immoral life. Neither Uncle Affleck nor her erstwhile prospective parents-in-law ever saw her again. She died in Charing Cross Hospital on 10th December 1981, of cirrhosis of the liver. She was just forty years old.

On his death Sir Robert left the whole of his by no means very large estate in trust for the endowment of a Hubert Agnew Fellowship in Metaphysics at Lincoln College, Oxford.

Should you ever wish to visit the haunts frequented by Imelda, Hubert and poor Superbo in happier days, let me repeat that you will be most welcome here at Fingleton Den. There is a spacious spare room here, with a small alcove where your little one could be put to rest. And may I wish you well for the prospective birth of the 'new little Agnew', as I hope your good husband will forgive my naming him, or perhaps her.
With every good wish,

Yours very sincerely,

Rufus G. Agnew.

7/35 Burnside Quadrant,
Bellshill,
Lanarkshire

11 May 1986

Dear Major Agnew,

It was very, very kind of you to take so much trouble and send me the photos and the family histories. I don't really know what to make of it all; I feel a bit shattered emotionally and besides a lot of it was probably above my head. 'Superbo' is a poor soul, isn't he? I hope they look after him well at the Royal Ed. I'm sure they do. Thank you for your last letter warning me not to make the wrong guesses about Superbo and my mother. I'm sure you're right that Hubert was my father, at least I like to think so he seems to have been a nice man. I don't understand that about Uncle Affleck's nickname, where is Uppingham? But I know all about cirrhosis of the liver, I don't like to think about that and I'm glad that you didn't tell me more.

I specially liked the photos which I am sending back to you by registered post. You don't have a spare one of my mother, do you? The funny thing is, of all the people in the photos the one I look most like is Uncle Affleck. Specially in the one taken when he was in his teens. I am enclosing a photo of myself and I am sure you will see the striking resemblance. It's strange, isn't it, how family likeness goes? Maybe I'm more an Affleck than an Agnew, but I suppose I'm a bit of both really.

It's very good of you to invite David and I to come and visit you, but we will soon be leaving Scotland. David has got promotion and is being moved to Nuneaton, we will be there by the time the baby is born. (If it is a girl, I shall call her Imelda.) But who knows, maybe some day . . .
Yours very sincerely,

Janice Moodie

Author's Note

In June 1986, Major Rufus Agnew, motivated by questions which had arisen in his mind on re-reading the memoirs of Frank Agnew and Sir Robert Affleck in the light of Mrs Janice Moodie's letter to him of 11th May that year, sought an interview with Dr Richard Downie, retired medical practitioner formerly practising in Duns. As a result of their discussions, Dr Downie subsequently made a statement to the G Division of Lothian and Borders Police. Following lengthy questioning of Dr Downie, of Frank Agnew–still a patient at the Royal Edinburgh Hospital–and of Mrs Jean Brumfitt, formerly cook at Lemington House, Frank Agnew was exonerated of all suspicion of involvement in the death of his brother Hubert. On July 29th, Dr Downie, then in his eighty-fifth year, died from a self-administered overdose of barbiturates.

Shortly after being interviewed by the police, Frank Agnew sent a long and confused letter to his cousin Rufus. Much of it is rambling and scarcely comprehensible; but in one of the more lucid passages the patient makes it clear that the obsessive idea of his responsibility for his brother's death was insinuated into his mind by Johnny Restorick, and suggests, perhaps wildly, that his mental collapse was precipitated by the tinker's having clandestinely drugged him with a hallucinogenic mushroom, possibly the Liberty Cap.

A further short passage seems worth quoting for the chill light which it sheds upon the hitherto obscure genesis of the family tragedy which has been unfolded. Recalling the dreadful occasion on which he came upon Sir Robert Affleck and his former batman so shamefully occupied in the stable, Superbo comments: 'The hateful tinker's voice, as I heard it unclearly in the moment before I advanced toward that scene of disgrace, has long haunted my memory and teased my understanding. As I believe I told you, the most I could make of his words at the time was the meaningless locution, 'And how good he upheld her.' In the light of what I now know, it has become horribly clear to me what I really heard that day. "And now," Restorick said to my uncle, "*you* be Imelda".'

On 5th September 1986, a warrant was issued for the arrest of John James Restorick, formerly employed as general handyman at Lemington House. It was alleged against him that 'on 24th November 1962 at Lemington House, near Duns, Berwickshire he did while acting along with Sir Robert Handyside Affleck, Bart., now deceased, formerly residing at Lemington House, administer a poisonous substance namely a poisonous mushroom to Hubert Blackadder Agnew formerly residing there and did cause said poisonous mushroom to be eaten by him and did murder him'.

Johnny Restorick was never apprehended. Early in 1987, acting on information received, Lothian and Borders Police began intensive searches of the grounds of Lemington Country House Hotel. It is believed that they were searching for the remains of John James Restorick, but nothing was found. The police file remains open.

Short Stories

The Disappearance of Ludmill Johnson

It can be a great strain always having to write stories that are full of meaning, so once in a while I like to write a story which has absolutely no meaning at all. Such a story is that of the disappearance of Ludmill Johnson, and it is a true story.

Ludmill Johnson's disappearance differed from most disappearances in that it was not entirely unexpected. He often used to say, 'Some day I shall disappear . . . '.

Ludmill Johnson lived alone and had always done so. (Perhaps not really always: as a child he had no doubt lived with his parents, but that had been a long time ago.) He had a sister in Auchterarder, but they did not get on.

Ludmill Johnson was knowledgeable in many subjects, but had never done anything at all throughout the whole of his life.

His disappearance was the more noteworthy and impressive as there was so much of him to disappear: 17 stone of corpulent geniality.

Conversation with Ludmill Johnson tended to be sparse and unrewarding.

'Good morning, Sir Ludmill.' (Ludmill Johnson was not a knight, but he liked to be called 'Sir Ludmill' and people tended to humour him. I would never go along with this at all, for it seemed to me grossly unfair to those who had taken the trouble to be knighted – and when I say unfair, I really mean downright immoral – that one who hadn't should be treated as if he had.)

'Fine morning, Sir Ludmill.'

'Well, er . . . not really.'

'Indeed, of course, very true . . . now that you come to mention it, Sir Ludmill, not so very nice at all . . . Terrible times we are living in, Sir Ludmill.'

'Yes, but perhaps marginally less awful than the fourteenth century.'

If, as might well be the case, his interlocutor knew nothing about the fourteenth century, the conversation would very likely come to an end at this point.

People often used to ask him about the origin of his name.

'That's very simple: son of John. John-son – son of John.'

'Yes . . . yes, of course . . . Really, I was thinking of your Christian name – Ludmill.'

'Ah, Ludmill! Masculine of Ludmilla.'

It seemed that really there must be more to it than that, but Ludmill Johnson gave the explanation with such peremptoriness and authority that no one dared to press him further on the matter.

It is a basic postulate of theology that God sustains all existent creatures in being. Should He withdraw His will from their being, they would thenceforth and instantaneously cease to be. Perhaps something of this sort happened to Ludmill Johnson. There was after all no reason why he should be sustained in being.

It was some time after breakfast one fine morning that Ludmill Johnson disappeared. Someone said to someone else, that afternoon,

'I haven't seen Ludmill Johnson today.'

'No, nor have I. We'd better look for him.'

They knocked at his door – no reply. They shouted through the letter-box:

'Are you there, Sir Ludmill?'

Again there was no reply, so they went in, and inside there was no sign of Ludmill Johnson. His bed had been slept in and his dirty breakfast dishes were on the table, which is why I asserted that he disappeared some time after breakfast, although in fact he had not been seen since early the previous evening.'

'He must be out,' said one person to the other.

'Yes, I suppose so,' the other replied, a little half-heartedly.

'Unless, of course, he's disappeared.'

'As he so often said that he would some day.'

'Exactly.'

Meaningful looks were exchanged.

And indeed he never reappeared. It is possible that he eloped with an extraordinarily silly old person called Mrs Fitou who had recently moved into the village. Everything about Mrs Fitou was silly – her name, her face, her conversation, her hats, everything; so it would be no surprise if she had chosen to go off with someone as pointless as Ludmill Johnson. But that is just a theory.

The Man Below

James Semple stared out of the window of the train with a kind of stubborn anxiety, contemplating in the glass the reflection of his own strong and dependable countenance, the one unchanging item within his view as sea, countryside and villages flicked disturbingly across his field of vision. He looked out of the window partly because he did not want to catch the eye of the unexceptional girl sitting opposite him (who, as a matter of fact, was not in the least interested in him, as she was simultaneously doing some kind of quick newspaper crossword and listing to tinny, disembodied music through earphones) and partly because the sight of the other passengers displeased him – a scruffy, undisciplined-looking lot, he thought, slack and noisy and surrounded by mess. He himself was dressed in an old but still respectable suit – which, however, he wore with an unaccustomed look – and a white shirt and tie, but he had opened the collar button and pulled his tie down a bit like a Yankee newspaper man in an old film.

Semple had already cracked his empty plastic coffee mug, causing the girl opposite to glance up momentarily in spite of her earphones, and now he was nervously scratching his knee under the table. He realised that he was in a disturbed state of mind, but acknowledged that it was not really surprising. Three days before he had been released from prison after serving eighteen years. When he had last seen the wide world – apart from journeys between different prisons – he had been twenty-two, and now he was forty. It was a long time.

The wide world had not, it seemed to him, changed for the better. He was appalled by the traffic, the noise, the mess and the general scruffiness; and it appeared that there were a lot more unsound, questionable-looking people around than there used to be. Moreover he had just spent a nightmarish two days in Dundee in the house of his married sister in Fintry, sleeping on the floor, getting in the way of a sullen and uncommunicative brother-in-law, hemmed in by loutish teenagers, menaced by yelling brats: his stay could not have been described as a success. He had determined almost at once to get out of the city as soon as he could; but it was an incident at the DSS which had precipitated his flight.

He thought of it as an incident, but really nothing had happened at all, nothing that could actually be pointed to or identified as an incident. For all that, there was no doubt that *something* had occurred, a confrontation, a challenge thrown out and accepted, a psychological face-off in which he had more than held his own – an 'inter-personal event', as some of those female prison psychologists would no doubt have termed it, of whom he so decidedly had the measure.

Semple had been patiently awaiting his turn, and had become aware of an argument going on between a man not far off from him and the official behind the desk. The man was tallish, dark, and from what Semple could see from his station in the rear, rather good-looking in a sinister, suspect kind of way. He seemed to be better-dressed than most of those in the place, and was arguing confidently, almost arrogantly, and without a hint of the subservience or deference often considered their due by DSS officials. Semple was not in the least interested in the content of the argument, but was beginning to accord the man a kind of tentative and provisional approval for the way he was conducting himself.

Quite suddenly, the man seemed to have carried his point: he stood up and turned away from the desk with an expression of triumph, of having outwitted the authorities. 'You look like Kafka,' thought Semple, invoking one of the writers he had become conversant with in prison. Just as this thought came into his mind, the man grinned broadly but somehow satirically, and nodded to Semple as if in acknowledgement of the thought. Simultaneously, the latter understood what it was that had made the other seem to him suspect or dubious: he was, undoubtedly, one of the Chosen Ones – something which, strangely enough, he had never held against Kafka. Semple stiffened and his eyes narrowed: he sat on tensely, unable to move as his turn had not yet come. The 'Jew-boy', as he now thought of him, moved away from the desk and joined two other men who were sitting to Semple's right, and whom he had previously scarcely noticed: now he shot a brief, hostile glance in their direction, and to his discomfiture saw them staring at *him* – all three were grinning in an insolent, provocative sort of way.

Semple turned his head away quickly. In the course of that swift exchange of looks he had divined something else: the men, all three of them, were homosexual. As he sat staring rigidly ahead of him, he felt their malevolent, insinuating stares. Those stares, he knew, were directed towards making him acknowledge an identity with their perverted unwholesomeness. He understood the malice of their insinuation, and he rejected it. For a couple of minutes, at least, he struggled with his acute discomfort and sense of outrage; then he half turned and stared back at them with a hard, cold look of contempt that made no concessions. He took careful stock of the three men. 'Kafka', the leader, was a cut above the other two, but they were all three of them unsavoury, malicious, shallow and untrustworthy people; just the kind, in fact, that he had done time for. Having exacted his taxation of contempt he turned and walked out of the building, his business forgotten.

Disturbed and disgusted by this experience, Semple made up his mind at once that he had had enough of the city. It was his loyalty to his race and his hatred of perversion and corruption which had stolen from him the best years of his life, and here he was again being confronted by all this same filth, the very moment he stepped back into the world. He was in a kind of controlled panic; and after returning to his sister's house to pick up his things he made straight for the station. Instinctively, he knew he had to head north, but being short of money he didn't want to go to Aberdeen, which was besides another city and doubtless a cesspool of corruption; so he bought a ticket for Montrose. It would have been cheaper to have travelled by bus, but the last time he had been in a bus he had been in handcuffs, and he was not anxious to stimulate that memory.

One vaguely apprehended reason for his choice of this destination was, paradoxically, that it lay in the general direction of Peterhead. Looking back, he now felt something almost akin to nostalgia for the earlier part of his sentence which he had spent there, when the prison had housed most of Scotland's hardest and most dangerous criminals. As he sat in the train gazing tensely out of the window his vivid recollections of all that began to rise unsought from the pool of memory, and he became gradually forgetful of his surroundings. It was an odd subject for nostalgia, that long, dour, grim struggle with authority and with himself, in which he had answered the brutality of the institution with his own brutality, waged a violent war against certain of his fellow-prisoners which was at the same time a shared war against the system, made himself feared and respected – respected, too, by authority itself in the end – and gradually climbed up the pecking-order. Through all that violence, fear and absurdity, that anger, despair and flickering hope, he had maintained his independence, his integrity and his self-respect. He had not softened or given in, he had refused to be moulded or modified, had emerged uncompromised and still his own man. It was an achievement of which he was quietly proud.

Long spells in the punishment cells had allowed him to make the acquaintance of his own mind. The rigours he was well able to withstand: like an ancient ascetic, a Desert Father, he had thrived on physical deprivation, retreated into the inner fortress of his self, and found there a grimly beautiful landscape, hard and merciless, unrelenting and all-enduring. He had discovered the world of books and education, acquainted himself with great writers and philosophers, gained eventually an Open University degree; but he had not let all that change him in his essence, he took what he wanted and jettisoned the rest. Out of all that had come one great legacy. Some prisoners discover Marx, or Nietzsche, or God: Semple discovered the Manichees and the Cathars.

He had stumbled upon the Manichees by chance, in a book about ancient history, found his imagination stirred, wanted to learn more. That had not proved easy, but he managed to pick up pieces of information here and there, and once he was on full-time education his access to books had vastly improved. So gradually Semple learned not only about the Manichees but about their forebears the Gnostics, and their heirs, the Cathars, and he imbibed their philosophy and embraced it to the extent of total identification. The dualist system fitted his temperament like a glove. To Semple it made the clearest sense that the world was born of the primeval contest between light and darkness, a contest in which darkness had prevailed, Satan had defeated God's champion, the Primal Man. So the world was an inextricable, blurred confusion of the light and the dark, but not an equal confusion, for the light was held down, imprisoned in matter, always at a disadvantage, always the underdog, vainly but pertinaciously striving to burst its chains, to escape from its bondage to contamination into the upper ether, the liberating world of spirit. And not only in the world as a whole, but in every individual being it was so: the light was in thrall, spirit held fast in matter, the ideal was sacrificed on the altar of the material.

In the light was God and in the darkness was Satan; and though Semple believed, in any strict sense, in neither the one nor the other, still it seemed to him that in the Manichaean symbolism was best expressed the struggle – engaged in always with the deepest pessimism – of the light to tear itself free of the darkness of the world and the body, to soar from this captivity to its heavenly home. And there were always a few, a chosen few, in whom this overcoming of the darkness could, in spite of everything, become reality. The Gnostics had called them the 'Spiritual', the Manichees the 'Elect', the Cathars the 'Perfect': they were those whose nature contained the divine spark, the hidden spark of spirit, the souls of fallen angels.

Apart from the loftiness of their philosophy, the beliefs and attitudes and way of life of these remote people held all kinds of subtle attractions for James Semple. He noted the hostility to the 'God of the Jews' which was a marked feature of the Gnostic sects, who often regarded him as the evil creator of the material world. He noted, too, that the Cathars had regarded the Catholic Church as an instrument of the Devil, the Prince of this World, and had rejected all its authority and its sacraments. He read with great interest and attention that many of the early sects had embraced 'Encratism', the rejection of marriage and sexuality. The rite of *abstinentia*, which for the Cathars freed the chosen ones from bondage and made them the Perfect, forbade sexual intercourse and the consumption of all the fruits of coition. The *Perfecti* led a rigid and sexless life of supreme austerity: they had the honour and distinction that came from their ability to carry a great burden, a burden that they exclusively could bear. So they were at the very head of the pecking-order.

Semple was convinced that successors to the Manichees and the Cathars must still exist in the modern world as a hidden, secret brotherhood. One need only look at history to see that this must be so. The basic dualist beliefs had passed down through the ages and they never died completely away. The Gnostics had passed on their heritage to the Manichees, who had been succeeded by the Paulicians and the Byzantine Bogomils; from them it had been transmitted to the Albigenses, the Cathars of the Middle Ages. Some historians had tried to deny that a direct line of transmission could be traced, but that was all guff: the beliefs of all these groups were too alike to have arisen spontaneously, and they were far too tough and durable to be persecuted out of existence. They must still exist underground, there was no doubt of that; but how were they to be found? Semple drummed his fingers nervously on the railway-carriage table: 'the devil's tattoo' he had heard that was called. Someone had told him that there was a course on the medieval heresies at St. Andrews University – perhaps the lecturers might know something. They might even be Cathars themselves.

Semple would find his way to the Cathars, sooner or later. He was determined: difficulties had never daunted him. Again and again in his life he had found his path blocked by the great boulder of reality, which would not countenance his high desire. Yet his dreams – which he believed allowed him to communicate with the divine spark within him – told him stubbornly that the reality of the ideal is undisturbed by the reality of the real. The reality of the ideal was therefore as *real* as that other reality, and might indeed be more real: so it seemed to him.

He recognised Montrose Basin: he had never been to the town, but he had studied a map before leaving, and there could be no mistaking the curious expanse of water, a little blob of the sea imprisoned by the land. At once he took down his canvas bag from the rack and, placing it on the table in front of him, sat with his arms folded protectively over it. Long before the train reached the station he stood up – now staring straight at the girl opposite him and, to his own surprise, smiling collectedly at her when she looked up – and made his way towards the door. Semple opened the window and stuck his head out with an impatient, searching, suspicious look, and jumped down while the train was still moving. He wasted no time in finding his bearings and began to walk quickly through the town in the direction of the sea, all the while throwing sharp, guarded glances about him as if he half expected to be ambushed at every close-mouth by hostile forces.

It was a sunny, warmish afternoon in early spring, but Semple was indifferent to it: he wanted only to find a room where he could shut himself in, be by himself and think. He followed signs pointing to the links and the beach, and soon found a suitable-looking guest-house. When he rang the bell a fair-haired, friendly girl of about seventeen appeared, and he asked if there was a room available for two or three nights. That would be no problem, she said, and he could have an evening meal if he wished.

'Do you work here?' he asked, casting about desperately for something to say.

'My Mum and Dad own it,' the girl replied. 'I'm Jackie, by the way.'

Semple stuck his head through the door of the lounge across from the desk, but a man was sitting there reading a newspaper, and he hastily withdrew. Then Jackie showed him to a small room on the top floor, overlooking a patch of garden and facing the backs of other houses. It was tidy and clean enough, with the curious qualification that the window sill was littered with a disconcertingly large number of dead flies. Semple viewed them with distaste but didn't know how to dispose of them, so he left them where they were. There seemed to be a lot of mirrors in the room: two were placed on opposite walls, producing endlessly receding images, while on the dressing table stood an old-fashioned glass with side-wings. Semple surveyed himself briefly and was not displeased with what he saw. The room was very warm and the heating was on; but instead of turning it off or opening the window he stripped off to his singlet, and having taken his shoes off and stowed them neatly under a chair, he lay down on the bed with his hands clasped behind his head, to think.

As his breathing rose and fell he squinted down at the tattoo which lurked among the curly brown hairs of his powerful chest: it showed a heart partly encircled by the motto AMOR VINCIT OMNIA. Semple, for all that, did not believe in love: when he had had that tattoo done it had been sex that he had had in mind. In fact, his few sexual encounters in the long-ago past of his freedom had all been brief, nasty and brutish. Jackie had left him a little disturbed, he had to admit. She was the type he would probably go for if he were going to go for women – fair, healthy-looking, perhaps a bit Scandinavian: he could well imagine her as the heroine of a Norse saga. But was he going to go for women? That was one of the problems he was going to have to confront. According to the ancient Manichees, Woman was the gift of the demons, who impelled men to progagate their kind in order that emancipation from matter and darkness might never come to them. He knew therefore that he ought, if he were to remain true to his principles, to keep himself inviolate.

He had been deeply hostile to the role of women in the prison system. All those female teachers, social workers, nurses, librarians and so on were there to soften and domesticate the prison population, to break down their solidarity and weaken their resolve. The weaker members, particularly, could easily be inveigled into opening their hearts to a woman, revealing their best-guarded secrets and, perhaps inadvertently, betraying their fellows. Whether they sought excitement and romance or merely a motherly bosom, he had seen them drop their guard, lower their defences and abandon all caution and reserve. Semple found it pitiful to observe notorious hard men creeping like lap-dogs into the bosoms of these women to be petted and fondled. He himself had never fallen victim to their wiles. He had not, of course, treated them with personal hostility, but had maintained an independence, a detachment, a reserve, and never for an instant sought from them anything beyond a strictly 'professional' relationship.

Semple drummed with his fingers on the back of his skull. He ought to have been considering the practicalities of his future, but preferred to concentrate on the more beguiling problem of making contact with the Cathars. Nothing new occurred to him, however, and before long he dropped off to sleep. Soon a dream came to him that was at first vague and confused: he was one of a group of prisoners, or perhaps army conscripts, under the power of tyrannical screws or NCOs. Twice the men revolted against the authorities and destroyed them. On the second occasion Semple led a group back to the barracks to confront a very evil-looking, martinet Negro NCO; to provoke him Semple marched and saluted with exaggerated, mocking, satirical efficiency. When the black reacted furiously they all set upon him and his fellows and beat them to death. That was very satisfying.

When he awoke he was sweaty and thirsty and had a slight headache. He washed his face in the basin with cold water, and after quite a struggle managed to get the window open. The atmosphere was really very oppressive; a half-dead fly was buzzing around the window, often falling down onto the sill among its deceased kin but always hauling itself up again; even with the window open it refused to go out. Semple supposed it must have been coaxed out of the woodwork by the warmth – it was really far too early in the season for flies to be buzzing everywhere in this irritating way. He wandered across to the mirror and again subjected himself to an inspection. His appearance had not suffered too severely from eighteen years inside: he was still strong and not overweight, his eye was as clear and commanding as ever. His face was a bit more lined, of course, and the hair had receded quite a bit, but that was nothing. He walked back to the window, watched the antics of the fly for a minute or two, thought of killing it but could not be bothered. Restlessly he turned back towards the mirror.

Semple stopped dead in his tracks. In the side mirror facing him stood the image of a man in a dark suit, with sleek black hair and a black moustache of the type worn by romantic film actors of the 1930s. He was not looking at Semple but gazing upwards as if at the ceiling, with a suspicious but at the same time slightly amused expression on his face. One hand was in his pocket, the other held a cigarette. A Dago type, Semple thought. He moved stealthily out of the sight of the mirror. In spite of the extreme shock which this untoward event had caused him, he kept a tight grip on himself and maintained his outward composure, because he felt somehow that he was under scrutiny. On no account must he be seen to panic: such a sign of weakness would put him at an immediate disadvantage. He was really more embarrassed than anything else by the whole thing. When the beating of his heart had stilled a little, he moved cautiously back within the range of the mirror. The man was gone: in his place he was happy to observe once more his own dependable countenance.

Semple sat down on his bed to consider the position. It did not take him long to reach the conclusion that he was the victim of some unaccountable invention which must have become fashionable while he was in prison: a new kind of mirror by means of which one could see what was going on in the room below, while the occupant of that room, perhaps, could spy on oneself. The outrageous unlikelihood of this hypothesis was not lost on him, but having once grabbed hold of it he hung on grimly. So his main defensive reaction to the curious happening was to pump up a sense of resentment at this uncalled-for assault on his privacy. He determined to speak to the proprietors about it, and got quite worked up over the issue, punching the palm of his hand in fury at the thought of the outrage that had been perpetrated on him.

Having dressed again in his shirt, tie and jacket he felt calmer and more his own man again. He went downstairs with the firm intention of making his views on the the subject of the mirror known to the proprietors, but when the nice Mrs Fordyce met him in the hall and told him in such a friendly way that the evening meal was about to be served, he felt somehow placated, as if his honour had been vindicated – goodness knows why – and decided to postpone his complaint. He had not, however, been sitting long in the dining room, the only other occupants of which were an unobtrusive old couple, when who should walk in but the man from the mirror, who was also, he realised at once, the same man who had been sitting in the lounge when he first arrived.

Semple stiffened and his eyes grew hard and fixed; but less because of the 'Dago' than on account of the woman who accompanied him. It could not be denied that she was striking. She too was dark, to the degree that Semple suspected her to have gypsy blood; she was of a stately carriage, cold in her expression though her eyes seemed to him to hold a veiled fire, and she was heavily made-up, her cheekbones rouged, her eyelashes black with mascara and the lids painted an ice-cold blue. She wore a black, close-fitting dress and very high heels, and her fingers flashed with jewellery. The Dago pulled out her chair with old-fashioned courtesy, and she sat down facing Semple, while her companion had his back to him. Almost immediately she measured Semple with a long, cool, provocative look; he managed to prevent himself from dropping his eyes and tried to look right through her at the wall behind, but he felt beads of sweat break out on his brow. The woman was pointedly appraising him, as if he were a sexual object.

The pair were thoroughly decadent and corrupt, of that there could be no doubt. They had a bottle of red wine brought to their table and, smoking throughout their meal, talked together in low, conspiratorial tones, the man leaning forward on his elbows with his face close to the woman's; words poured from him ceaselessly while she watched him closely, intently, but all the while scarcely allowing the ghost of a smile to animate the chill immobility of her features. From time to time – whenever, in fact, her companion's attention was momentarily engaged elsewhere – she gazed insolently over at Semple in a manner the directness of which could easily imply contempt. Jackie was serving the meal, and he felt towards her an almost humble gratitude for her contrasting healthy normality, her Nordic ruddiness, the friendly smile that seemed to anchor him in a clean, wholesome world, a world in which one could look into a mirror and be confident of meeting one's own gaze.

The Dago's woman reminded him insistently of someone. He was already on his apple crumble when the recognition came to him: it was the stepmother, the witch, the Wicked Queen in the film of *Snow White*. When he was a child of about five he had gone to see the film with his granny, and whenever the Wicked Queen appeared on the screen his granny would say, 'Dinnae look, dinnae look the noo, Jimmy, cover yer eyes, son . . . '. Jimmy had dutifully gone through the motions but peeked surreptitiously between his fingers, proud to be out-facing terror and evil.

But now, in the face of the woman's repeated hard stare, Semple wanted only to escape. At the first possible moment he stood up, turned abruptly and walked out of the dining room. He went straight up to his room, locked the door, and was at once overcome by a weariness passing any he had ever before experienced. He was barely capable of undressing and climbing into bed, and as soon as he lay down and turned out the light he was instantly asleep. Sometime during the night he had the following fearful dream.

Jackie, lovely, blonde little Jackie, was in the power of a malign creature. This creature was blue-green in colour, scaly, something like a crocodile or alligator in form with a long, pointed snout but standing upright. Jackie stood meekly before it, hanging her head. The monster took what appeared to be a hypodermic needle and pierced her wrist, then performed the same operation on itself, and rubbed their two wrists together, mingling the blood. This, the dreamer understood, would infect Jackie with some vile venom or virus. She submitted without protest, with sad, downcast eyes. The only hope now was an antidote, but how could she receive it in time? A number of people were in the vicinity but none of them came to her aid; they made a pretence of not noticing, but this was palpably and almost insultingly unconvincing. Semple was appalled by his own impotence – in a panic he cast round for help, but none was to be found, he and Jackie were entirely alone in the cruel world of the malign green monster . . . .

He awoke early, deeply disturbed by his repellent dream. It had left him with one very strong and important impression: that the vile creature which had so wickedly infected Jackie represented the Wicked Queen, the Dago's woman. This was one of those dream associations whose validity could not be doubted, though the only physical suggestion of identity lay in the monster's colour, which associated with the woman's eye make-up. The message conveyed by the dream was that the Wicked Queen was maliciously disposed towards Jackie, and intended to do her some evil. Semple's protective instincts bristled at the thought, and stirred him to outrage. But he was astute enough to understand that to arouse such emotions might well be the woman's purpose: by stirring up his feelings for Jackie she might be aiming indirectly at his sexual enthralment. He realised that in his present situation he was intensely vulnerable to the machinations of the Powers of Darkness. Potentially, at least, he was one of the elect, the perfect, the unsullied ones. That dark forces would seek to subvert his will was to be expected. His first task was to work out what exactly was the nature of their game.

This presented him with a psychological challenge. In prison, the various issues of honour in which he had become involved had always been clear-cut, and decisive physical action had been what was required to put matters right, to restore the lost balance. There would be practical, logistical problems to solve, but these belonged in the concrete everyday world and solutions to them could be found there. Semple was accustomed to responding to challenges with physical, and generally violent, action, but he realised that there might be unpredictable complications involved in a square-go with the Prince of Darkness. He did not mind playing a waiting game if he knew what he was waiting for: but now the enemy's intentions were frustratingly obscure, and their methods altogether outside his experience.

For all that he was, this morning, in a more positive frame of mind. He had a cold shower and was the first down to breakfast, and, eating fast, had finished before the appearance of his sinister neighbours. The day was fine and spring-like, and donning an old donkey jacket he set off to walk up the links. He wanted to allow his thoughts room to move and adjust, to dispel with exercise the clouds of perplexity.

He returned in mid-afternoon, once more frustrated and on edge. At first he had found the open air bracing and stimulating to his thoughts, and with a broad stretch of time before him felt confident that the solution to his dilemma would come to him spontaneously. But as he walked and his thoughts revolved, he realised that they were doing only that, revolving constantly without reaching a terminus, whirling fruitlessly round upon their

axis. What *was* his dilemma, anyway? It had no graspable substance, nothing to give him a mental toehold. He began to find all
the unaccustomed space around him oppressive and vaguely
threatening. There was also a specific irritant: a dog, a nasty,
mankie-looking mongrel tyke, attached itself to him and refused
to be driven off. It stuck with him, trotting a little behind, circling
and straying and returning, when he turned back towards the
town, and he eventually succeeded in shaking it off only by going
into a café where he ate a couple of pies and drank a mug of tea.
Reluctant to return to the guest-house, he wandered about aimlessly for some time until the longing to be enclosed asserted itself
once more.

Back in his room, Semple went to bed and slept. He dreamt that
he had gone to sleep in a garden in some tropical land. He woke
(in his dream) to the awareness that a huge snake lay coiled heavily
at the back of his neck – he could feel and hear it sucking away
at his nape. The horror of the dream awoke him in reality: the
duvet was caught under his shoulder, preventing him from
turning over. Such was the vividness of the impression, though,
that to his shame he actually looked under the bed to make sure
there was no basis in fact for that overwhelming sense of an alien,
malevolent presence.

Some time later, getting himself ready to go down for the
evening meal, Semple opened the drawer of the dressing-table in
which he had stowed a few clothes and other items, and found,
not his own things, but someone else's. There were a couple of
shirts, two or three ties, a razor in an imitation leather case, a pair
of nail scissors – none of them had he ever laid eyes on before. He
banged the drawer shut furiously. They were trying to get rid of
him, had started to clear his stuff out when he was absent, had
installed someone else in his place! What did this mean, what was
it all about?

His bag was still on the rack, other of his things still lying about
the room. He opened further drawers – his missing belongings
were not there, nor had they been put into his bag. He re-opened
the first drawer, meaning to throw the alien items out into the
passage. It was empty. His heart leapt into his throat, but at the
same time a voice within said, 'Don't panic. Don't give yourself

away.' Cautiously, experimentally, Semple closed the drawer again, quietly, then opened it once more. His own possessions were there just as he had left them.

He sat down heavily, feeling faint, and dropped his head between his knees. 'This must be what it is like to be mad,' he thought, 'and to know that you're mad.' When he had recovered a little he had a curiosity to see for himself how ghastly the shock must have made him appear, so he stood up and looked in the mirror, which had played no more tricks since the previous evening. A fresh horror met his eyes. His body was there, clear and solid, but his face and head were virtually invisible. Only a vague shadow subsisted, a kind of opaque blur, which even as he watched thinned, faded and disappeared, leaving nothing. And by now, his body was suffering the same fate as his face – it began to lose definition, it became fuzzy and indeterminate, it faded and dissolved. The mirror now reflected only the room. Semple turned away in bitterness and despair but, unable to restrain himself, turned back once more towards the mirror. A solid form was there once more, but just for a fleeting second it seemed to be someone else, with a coarse face and reddish-fair hair and moustache, like a fellow-prisoner at Peterhead whom he had particularly detested. This impression passed so rapidly that it might have been illusory, and the mirror again showed himself, James Semple, haggard, his face grey and sweating, his eyes at once fascinated and fearful – but indubitably himself.

Semple did not waste much time in questioning his own sanity. Something objective had happened to him, though something which lay quite outwith the laws of nature. He knew himself enchanted, and he knew the source of his enchantment: the Dago's woman, the Wicked Queen, had bewitched him. He was fighting the Powers of Darkness, and perhaps for his life – maybe for Jackie's life, too. To overcome terror, he conjured up anger. He was furious at his own incapacity to act – but how did one deal with the Prince of this World? Inaction was unbearable, the need to react physically almost overpowering. In bitter frustration, he violently punched his left palm with his right fist. The rich, violent slamming sound fortified his soul.

In the dining room, when the infernal pair had taken their

places, the previous evening's provocation was repeated. The woman would glance over at him every now and again, her features still cold and hard, but on some occasions now shamelessly smiling, a smile that was at once mocking and come-hither, suggestive yet derisive of his manhood. Semple felt himself taunted, dared to prove himself a man. The woman was insinuating that his independence, his self-containment and self-sufficiency, his heroic austerity of life, were not that at all, but something else, something weak and impotent and disgraceful, something unnamably decadent and corrupt ... The man of the mirror seemed unaware of the attentions she was paying Semple. He continued to speak all the time in a low voice, bending towards the woman, sometimes fondling her hand. Semple stared back at her with cold fury; but just once, as he was about to rise from the table, he answered her smile with his own, with a smile which said what *he* had to say, a smile that was delivered on his own terms and with his own very particular meaning.

To his surprise, Semple slept well that night. He awoke aware of sunshine in the room; aware, too, of a curious pervasive buzzing, which at first he sleepily took for an electric razor or perhaps a hair drier in the next room. But as his consciousness cleared he understood that the sound was altogether less innocent. With great apprehension he raised himself on an elbow and peered in the direction of what now seemed a seething commotion. On the chair where he had laid out his clothes, his briefs were hanging, but they appeared to have turned black: for they were crawling and swarming, almost to invisibility, with huge, fat, vicious-looking flies. The flies were nowhere else – only buzzing, seething and swarming over this single item of underwear. Semple was utterly unnerved: this was far more terrible than anything else that had happened to him in that deceptively ordinary-looking room. For at least a minute, he sat paralysed with disgust, his spirit cowed. Then, with a kind of roar, he leapt from his bed, grabbed a towel, and started thrashing and flailing at the flies with uncontrollable rage, not letting up until almost all of them were dead. Then, panting and gasping, he gingerly picked up the briefs between finger and thumb, and, close to retching, deposited them in the wastepaper basket.

The Dago and his woman were already seated at breakfast when Semple came into the dining room. He did not look at them. After some time Mrs Fordyce, who was serving breakfast, was called away to the phone; and almost at once the Dago rose to leave, while the woman remained sitting, her elbows on the table, cradling her coffee cup in her hands. Semple glanced up, and as he passed Semple's table the Dago, smiling familiarly, nodded to him, just as if he were saying that the way was now clear, that the woman was all his. So Semple looked straight at the woman – though he would have preferred to keek at her from between his fingers – and she was smiling at him blatantly, a shameless invitation in her corrupt, calculating, foreign-looking eyes. Semple stood up, remained for a moment gazing at her, then started to walk in the direction of her table; but before reaching it he swerved and went through the door leading to the kitchen.

There Jackie, in a dirty apron, was washing up. She turned from her work, surprised, as Semple walked in, and blushing a little, asked him if he needed more coffee. He shook his head vaguely, looking around him, then smiled foolishly, shuffled his feet, and looked as if he would like to talk. But he recollected himself, his eyes shone hard, and he looked around once more, this time with intent, and saw what he wanted. He picked up a bread knife, tested it with his thumb, and walked purposefully back with it into the dining room.

The Day I Met the Queen Mother

That day started just like any other day. I got up, washed, had my breakfast, caught the bus to work. How could I possibly have known that before I got back into bed that night, I would have met the Queen Mother?

The lower deck of the bus was full up as usual, so I climbed upstairs and established myself on one of the seats at the front end which are designated as a No-Smoking area. We had not travelled the distance of one stop when a man sitting in front of me, wearing a great big flowery hat, took a packet of cigarettes from his pocket and lit up! I tapped him lightly on the shoulder, and when he turned round I pointed wordlessly at the No-Smoking sign on the window beside him. He turned away and continued smoking for about half a minute in order not to lose face; then he dropped his cigarette on the floor, stubbed it out with his toe and left his seat, remarking as he went, 'I think I'll go somewhere where the company is pleasanter.'

'Who in the name of God was that?' I asked a decent, sensible-looking, middle-aged woman sitting across from me, for I was surprised by his attitude.

'That's the Queen Mother,' she replied.

You could have knocked me over with a feather! That was not what I thought the Queen Mother was like at all – either in manners or appearance! In the first place the man looked about forty-three, whereas the Queen Mother is an old thing of about ninety. Then he might well have been a queen, uncapitalised, but a mother, even lower-case, scarcely! Unlike the Q.M., again, he had a long angular, grey face, and was dressed in a scruffy, grubby, stained anorak. Indeed the only thing he had in common with the said gracious lady was his enormous flowery hat.

It occurred to me, therefore, that my informant might be insane, and had concluded merely from the fact that the man was wearing a big flowery hat, that he must be the Queen Mother. It is a well-known failing of the insane to take a mere adjunct or accident as a defining characteristic. In my childhood I learned from my mother that our lunatic asylums are filled with mentally disturbed persons who can be divided into two principal categories: those labouring under the impression that they are Napoleon, and those, seated on pieces of toast, who believe themselves to be poached eggs. For our present purposes the first category is irrelevant and can be forgotten. But what an extraordinary thing, I always felt, to conclude simply from the fact that one happened to be sitting on a piece of toast, that one must be a poached egg! After all, compared to a poached egg a human being is very large in relation to the average slice of toast. And again, many other things can rest on a piece of toast – baked beans, for instance, or tinned spaghetti, to name but two! However, many mentally sick people are also deficient in imagination.

But wait, I hear you protest, are you not overlooking something? May it not be, you ask, that these people do not believe themselves to be poached eggs merely because they happen to find themselves sitting on a slice of toast, but, on the contrary, they sit on toast because they believe themselves to be poached eggs? And you are right, for it was this objection precisely that now occurred to me! And, applying this insight to the case of the Queen Mother, we would have to conclude that it was more likely to be the man in the hat than the sensible-looking woman who was insane; because although the latter might have insanely concluded, from the fact that the man was wearing the hat, that he was the Queen Mother, the obverse deduction – that because he was the Queen Mother he must therefore be wearing the hat – cannot, in her case, be made meaningful. But if we assume the *man* to be insane, the conclusion is very different. What more unlikely than that he should assume, merely because he was wearing a big flowery hat, that he was the Queen Mother? – for many other people, besides the said gracious lady, though admittedly less famous, wear big

flowery hats. If, on the other hand, he already believed himself
to be the Queen Mother, what could be more natural – more
inevitable, one might even say – than that he should, to enforce,
as it were, the identity, don just such a headgear?

Yes, but . . . granted that the man could be insane, was it likely
that such a decent and sensible-looking woman would simply
have taken him at his word on such a dubious claim? Sometimes
I almost wonder if I may not be going a little crazy myself – could
I just have imagined it all?!! No, but seriously . . . if you are really
looking for something to give me for my birthday (although, as
I keep saying, I really don't want *anything*), I can think of nothing
I'd like more than *The Bumper Book of Queen Elizabeth the Queen
Mother*.

The Devil and Dr Tuberose

Dr Marcus Tuberose was being victimised. Whether it was because he had a poetic temperament, or because of his present difficult domestic circumstances, or because of the machinations of Dr Philip Pluckrose, his rival and enemy, or whether all these factors were fatally combining to discredit and disadvantage him, was not yet clear. An artistic sensibility, he well knew, was not a recommendation in the world of academic departmental politics; rather it was a focus of jealousy, suspicion and mistrust. Dr Tuberose did not flaunt his superiority in the very least; but neither on the other hand did he attempt hypocritically to conceal it. He knew his worth, and he knew that some day that worth would be recognised. But his openness in this respect did put him at a disadvantage, he was well aware of that. He did not conceal that from himself, not at all.

The fact that he had recently been deserted by his wife, Malitia, did not help either. The break-up of a marriage might no longer be in itself a social embarrassment, but in this case the circumstances, the particular and special circumstances . . . Dr Tuberose was not unconscious of the fact that there were people who did not scruple to laugh at him behind his back. People were like that, and academics in particular were like that. Dr Tuberose knew that he had not always made himself popular. He spoke his mind when it would be against his conscience to keep silent, and that was not a worldly-wise thing to do. But he thanked God that worldly wisdom had never been a part of his make-up. He was also not adept at currying favour in high places, unlike certain successful departmental politicians he could think of. It was amazing, he always thought, how intelligent people were so easily taken in by flattery. But then vanity was a powerful force, a more powerful force than intelligence, or disinterested commitment, a much stronger force than honesty or intellectual integrity . . . that was the way the world was, the way it had always been.

Ever since it had become known that Professor McSpale was to spend the coming academic year at the University of Delaware, a certain sentence had kept revolving and repeating itself in Dr Tuberose's head. He had not exactly composed it, it had come as it were unbidden and without his full consent. These things happened to people of a poetic sensibility, of an intuitive temperament, they were not altogether under conscious control. 'Marcus Aurelius Tuberose, MA, B Litt, Ph D, has been appointed Acting Head of the Department of English Literature for the academic year 1988–89.' That was the little sentence, or jingle. It was silly, he knew – he was even a little ashamed of it, deep down. But, after all, the message which it contained communicated an essential truth. The formal recognition which that sentence would represent, should it ever emerge from the mind of Dr Tuberose into outer reality, would be no more than he deserved. He did not expect it or ask for it, he disdained to canvas it or tout for it or flatter for it, but he was too honest to hide from himself the simple fact that he deserved it. Not that he wanted it, no, but simply that he deserved it.

A month ago it had seemed to him that it was really going to happen. Things were looking good, he felt, he was not blind to the impression that there were certain factors in his favour, certain realities which it would be foolish to ignore, unrealistic, in a sense, to disregard . . . Then had come the day of the departmental meeting. Dr Tuberose had arrived early, but Philip Pluckrose was there before him, and so, strange to say, was Professor McSpale. Dr Tuberose did not like the smell of that. They were huddled deep in conversation when he entered, McSpale expatiating assertively but in low, almost conspiratorial tones, Pluckrose nodding vehemently, but with a look of fawning obsequiousness that was quite revolting. When Tuberose entered the room they ceased their confabulations quite suddenly, even blatantly, as if scorning to conceal the truth that they had been saying things that were not for his ears, things that were almost certainly to his direct disadvantage.

The decision as to the appointment of the Acting Head of Department was, as it turned out, deferred until the next meeting. Tuberose did not like that, it was clear to him that it meant that whatever understanding was being worked out between McSpale and Pluckrose required time to be brought to fruition, that it was unscrupulously being given time, and that time was therefore on the side of his enemies. During the course of that afternoon, he was frequently aware of Professor McSpale directing at him, from under his coarse, tangled, greying eyebrows, a quite peculiar look. It was a look that, thinking about it afterwards, he found it very hard to analyse. It was a look of scorn, perhaps, of hard, cold scorn, and there was something insolently defiant about it, something altogether blatant. It seemed to say that power was going to be exercised, directly and shamelessly, that justice and right were going to be disregarded, trampled upon, set altogether at nought, that this was wrong, yes, certainly, but it was going to happen all the same, and there was nothing whatever that Dr Tuberose could do about it, not this time. This, Tuberose realised, was the price of integrity, this was the cost of speaking one's mind.

Ever since that meeting the attitude of condescending friendliness which Philip Pluckrose customarily adopted towards him had become more odiously bland, and at the same time more unconcealedly tinctured with genial contempt. On one occasion he had even had the effrontery to pretend to commiserate with Tuberose about his domestic misfortune. 'You'll have to come and have a meal with Polly and I,' he had fawned with his customary grammatical insensibility, 'and if there is anything we can do to help, Marcus, you know we're always at the end of the phone . . .' – and so on and so on; it would be embarrassing to record all the banal, gloating hypocrisies that oozed from his lips and hung heavily in the air like halitosis.

But Dr Tuberose's nature was not of the kind that lies down meekly under persecution. He had, of course, the clean bright shield of conscious integrity with which to defend himself, but he had something else too, something more tellingly substantial, an eloquent expression of his worth that would be hard for anyone simply to ignore, even the hardened careerists of the department, to whom intellectual distinction was apparently such a contemptible irrelevance in the primitive struggle for place, power and personal advantage. This secret weapon was his new lecture course on the Romantic Imagination, which was to form the nucleus, the matrix, of his projected work on this well-worn topic. Already, in spite of himself, Dr Tuberose could hear phantom phrases from future critical comments on this embryonic work of genius flitting restlessly about his brain: 'allusive, learned, lucid and perspicacious'; 'the daring taxonomies of Tuberose'; 'as Tuberose has seminally suggested'; and so on and so forth.

Everything, however, depended on the success of the lecture course, really everything. Dr Tuberose was now in such a position and of such an age that if he didn't go up, he could only go down – or even out. Things being as they were in the academic world, it was either promotion or early retirement, Tuberose knew that. Since the most recent departmental meeting he was aware, too, that the odds were stacked heavily against him. But the lecture course might yet change all that. There were some things that simply couldn't be disregarded, even by the English department, one had to believe that, or else life could hold no meaning.

In the early hours of the morning of the day, a Friday, on which he was due to deliver his first lecture in the series, Dr Tuberose awoke in his lonely bed moaning and groaning from a most appalling nightmare. He had entered through the sliding doors of the main arts building of the university, his lecture notes in his briefcase, to find himself, without surprise, in the chamber of the House of Commons. A vast crowd composed of students, newspaper correspondents, internationally famous critics, and even a few well-known movie stars, was wedged closely in the benches and thronging eagerly in the aisles, jostling for position, manifesting every symptom of impatient excitement, awaiting in breathless anticipation some crucial public announcement. As the bewildered Tuberose mingled with the throng, an official in the shape of a Himalayan bear advanced towards the Speaker's chair, followed by Professor McSpale in the garb of the Lord Chancellor. The Himalayan bear banged three times on the ground with his ceremonial staff and called for silence. Professor McSpale, instantly picking out Tuberose among the seething press, fixed him for a terrible moment with a baleful eye flashing with a most hellishly malignant lustre. Then he averted his gaze, and drawing from among the folds of his gown a slip of paper, read out in clear and ringing tones: 'Philip Endymion Pluckrose, MA, D Phil, has been appointed Acting Head of the Department of English Literature for the academic year 1988–89.'

A wild cheer rose up, and almost instantly every eye was turned upon Dr Tuberose with open, wicked mockery, while raucous laughter burst out and jeers, whistles and catcalls smote upon his ears. He dropped his head in shame and struggled to leave, but no one would let him pass; instead they shoved and shouldered him provocatively while heaping upon him vague but deadly insults. Then Professor McSpale pointed to him with his long, lank, skinny finger, slapped the Himalayan bear on the rump and shouted, 'Go get him, Spielberg!' The crowd instantly parted, and the bear charged down the aisle towards Dr Tuberose with slavering fangs, and there was nowhere for him to flee. Its teeth were not a hair's-breadth from his throat when the unhappy scholar awoke in the pitiable condition already indicated. For the remainder of that night he tossed and turned hopelessly as fragments of his lecture, the announcement by Professor McSpale, the superior smile of Pluckrose, the teeth of the Himalayan bear and the inscrutable eyes of a certain Chinese waiter mingled and coalesced in the fevered jumble of his imagination.

It may be imagined that Dr Tuberose entered the lecture hall considerably unnerved. He was made of stern stuff, however, Marcus Aurelius Tuberose was not a man of jelly, and in spite of every setback he remained quietly but ruthlessly determined to do himself justice, to acquit himself with honour, to put all his cards squarely on the table, to show up Pluckrose for what he was. In this first lecture he was plunging right into the very heart of the matter, addressing Coleridge's distinction between Fancy and Imagination. As he warmed to his subject he began to be stirred and even exalted by his own eloquence, and he was soon confident that he had his audience eating out of the palm of his hand. The tables were turned, Pluckrose was a dead letter – even in the impetuous onrush of his discourse that consciousness was shining at the back of his mind. And then a terrible thing happened.

'We have, above all, to ask ourselves,' Dr Tuberose was saying as he reached what he thought of as the high point of his lecture, 'what exactly Coleridge meant by "Imagination". We have to be clear about this before we can proceed any further. Did he mean by "Imagination" a permanent, universal faculty of the human mind, equally possessed by all? Or did he mean by it what we nowadays usually understand the term to mean, namely a mere image-forming capacity, an ability to image to ourselves facts and possibilities and potentialities outside immediate reality, a capacity which different people possess in differing and variable degrees? Do we all possess Imagination in the same way in which we all possess two arms and two legs?'

Dr Tuberose paused impressively and looked around at his audience. He was about to continue when he noticed a hand raised about three-quarters of the way up the lecture hall, to his right, near a side-entrance. To his irritation, and with a certain sinking of the heart, he saw that it belonged to an unhealthy-looking young man in a wheelchair, the lower moiety of whose person was concealed by a travelling-rug.

'Yes?' he snapped impatiently, in a way which he hoped indicated that interruptions were not scheduled for this lecture course.

'Excuse me,' came back at him the weak but at the same time assertive tones of the student in the wheelchair, 'but it is not true that we all possess two arms and two legs.'

Dr Tuberose frowned and traversed the rostrum once or twice, looking at his feet.

'Let me re-phrase that,' he resumed. 'Do we all possess Imagination in the same way in which we all possess a head?' He paused again. 'Or am I once again assuming too much? Is there anyone here without a head?'

This sally was met with a horrified, stunned silence.

'So,' said Dr Tuberose complacently, 'we all have heads.' He paused yet again. 'But perhaps there is among us some smart-ass with *two* heads, who would like to exploit his – or, I had no doubt better add, her – misfortune in order to score a debating point off me?'

At this, signs of disorder began to manifest themselves in the lecture hall: there was some laughter of a nervous kind, but also more ominous stirrings and mutterings. Dr Tuberose raised his voice.

'I can see that I shall have to make a diversion, in order to attempt to establish the distinction between essence and accident. The essence of a thing refers to that which it is in itself, its inner, universal condition; its accidents refer to that which has befallen it accidentally, that, in other words, which has *happened* to it. The essence of a thing is undisturbed by its accidents.'

'It wasn't an accident!' shouted the student in the wheelchair, 'I was born without legs!'

'You misunderstand me!' yelled back Dr Tuberose, 'you misunderstand me deliberately and maliciously! That you were born without legs is an accident, essentially you have legs! I will not be provoked! I will not be persecuted!'

Scarcely aware of what he was doing, shaking with fury but also close to tears, he began gathering up his papers and stuffing them into his briefcase. There was a vague consciousness in him that he was crossing some kind of Rubicon, that he was recklessly hurling himself forward into a region whence there is no return, but he did not care, the ardour and impetuosity of his temperament carried him onwards and could not be withstood; and then he was right, right beyond a shadow of doubting, persecuted and provoked and buffeted by the tempests of ill-fortune, but right, right, right ... The students were too shocked to move or speak, they sat on in wide-eyed amazement, although a few were tentatively standing up, it was hard to say why. Dr Tuberose tore out of the lecture hall, made straight for the staff toilet and plunged his head in a basin of cold water.

He could just not account for this unprovoked attack. He was aware that he was liberal even to a fault, entirely confident that his record was irreproachable. He had always, as it happened, had particularly compassionate feelings and views about the treatment of the limbless. Had he not, as a matter of fact, been directly responsible, through his forceful eloquence at a crucial meeting of the University Council, for the installation of ramps and electrically-operated sliding doors throughout the lecture block –

was it not through his caring vigilance that the very ramp existed by which his assailant had ascended to his commanding position above Dr Tuberose? And was this his reward? More, had he not agitated, unsuccessfully it was true but sincerely, for the removal from the University Library of all shelves higher than three feet from the ground? And how was he now rewarded?

But when at length he emerged from the toilet, everything became instantly and chillingly clear. Little groups of students from his truncated lecture were standing around in animated conversation, there was a general buzz of excited gossip and speculation, there was seriousness and there was laughter, there was a little hilarity but perhaps a great deal more righteous indignation. Around the student in the wheelchair a particularly large and vocal group had gathered, and among them, with a lunge of panic, a stab of recognition and at the same time a detached, ironical insight, a kind of sigh of inevitability, he identified the little Mephistophilean beard and the brown corduroy jacket of Philip Endymion Pluckrose. Tuberose realised now, with a calm certainty, that all this had been planned long ago. A student had been suborned, his lecture course deliberately sabotaged, and it was, of course, precisely this that McSpale had been plotting with Pluckrose on the afternoon of the departmental meeting.

Tuberose gazed at his enemy with a disgust too deep for words. Pluckrose always looked to him as if he were in disguise, like a spy in a bad comedy film of the fifties. The ascetic cut of his meagre, jet-black hair suggested a renegade monk of the Renaissance, despatched on some obscure and dubious mission to a distant court – an aspiring poisoner, perhaps; while his black trimmed beard gave the impression of being hooked over his ears. The truth, thought Tuberose, was that Pluckrose *was* in disguise: hiding himself, masking the truth of his own malice and hopeless mediocrity, poisoning the minds of the young, poisoning the wells of truth, poisoning them all against Tuberose, the righteous one, the disinterested one, the man of integrity. Pluckrose the poisoner.

There had to be a confrontation, Tuberose knew that, but not yet. Now was not the time. The students were incensed, they had been stirred up against him, bought by Pluckrose, and he could hope for no justice there. But tonight he would speak out – yes, tonight at Cowperthwaite's party. Everybody in the department would be there, everybody who counted, anyway, with one crucial exception. McSpale, he knew, had been obliged to refuse the invitation, or at least had made some excuse, and that was greatly in the favour of Dr Tuberose. Without McSpale, Pluckrose was nothing, a mere paper tiger, a hand puppet from which the hand had been withdrawn, essentially just a limp rag. In fact, to call Pluckrose a limp rag was to flatter him.

When Tuberose had said what he had to say, Pluckrose would be finished, it would be totally out of the question that he could become Acting Head of the Department, he would be obliged instead to apply for early retirement, and he would be lucky if he got that, very lucky indeed. In fact he would be much more likely to be up before the University disciplinary committee, a fate normally reserved for only the most hopeless drunks, and he might even have to leave the country. And then, of course, Tuberose would come into his own. His worth would be recognised, his disinterested and fearless exposure of Pluckrose would be widely discussed and favourably assessed, integrity would win through, truth would prevail and poetic sensibility be vindicated, he would be appointed Acting Head of Department, the idea of a personal Chair would be mooted, his book on the Romantic Imagination would be praised by George Steiner, he would succeed McSpale, and so on and so forth . . . .

What happened to Dr Tuberose between the truncation of his lecture and the time of his arrival at the Cowperthwaites' party, I do not know. He was known not to be a heavy drinker, and had he over-indulged himself on this occasion it would have been quite out of character. On the other hand, a man of his delicate frame, and of a constitution unaccustomed to alcohol, might, I suppose, have been more affected than another by a little Dutch courage. But those present at the party all agreed that Dr Tuberose did not really appear to be drunk. It is more likely that his susceptible and excitable temperament was agitated by his horribly disturbed night, by the most unfortunate incident which had interrupted so inauspiciously the first in his series of lectures, and by the rather fevered speculations outlined above. He had, besides, been under considerable strain for some time past as a result of his unfortunate domestic circumstances; and that, really, is as much as can be usefully suggested as likely to throw light on what follows.

Everybody enjoyed the little gatherings given once or twice a year by Cowperthwaite and his lovely wife, Aminta. Cowperthwaite was a remarkable man. His favourite word was 'teleological', though he was pretty keen also on 'ontological', 'epistemological' and 'taxonomy'. He was always calling his children 'darling' and his wife 'sweetheart', and sometimes he would even address the family dog, Demiurge, as 'darling'. Aminta was not quite as intelligent as her husband, though not, of course, by any means unintelligent. Perhaps for this reason, she was a stabilising influence on the wilder flights of Cowperthwaite's speculative conjectures. She spoke to him habitually in a teasing tone which conveyed that for all his little weaknesses there was really no one in the world quite so wonderful as he. That is not to say that he was not at times an embarrassment to her: when on one dire occasion that evening, he spoke of the 'Heraclitean flux', her reaction was such as to suggest that she had mistaken that ontological phenomenon for a form of dysentery.

Demiurge, who is to play a not unimportant part in this tale of truth, was a cross between a spaniel and a corgi, something that can't possibly be imagined until it has been seen. As to his name, he was the victim of some obscure academic joke, a fate which, along with his appearance, probably contributed to his habitual look of shame, as if he were the author of some vile mess on the carpet which was perpetually the subject of discussion. Though known familiarly in the household as 'Demmy', he seemed to know that this was merely a diminutive, and to live in constant fear that the guilty secret of his full name would be revealed to visitors; as, indeed, it often was, thanks to his master's keenness to tell the story attached to the name, which displayed his genial intelligence to especial advantage.

I wish I could describe the wit and urbanity and the relaxed intellectual authority which marked the tone of that memorable

evening: the talk of contemporary film, of child abuse, of
advanced social theory, of construction and deconstruction, of
Adorno and Jürgen Habermas, of 'the Frenchman, Derrida'
(whose name I personally would have pronounced 'Dereeda', but
whom all of that company, and certainly correctly, called 'Derry
Dah'); and at the same time the common touch, the homely
aspersions on the Thatcher Government, the substitution of the
word 'Jockish' for 'Scottish', and other little foibles to which it
would be unpardonably bad taste to draw attention; and then the
sense almost of an extended family, united in benignity and
complacency of feeling, in the best sense: all this I would love to
be able to depict. But my talents are not equal to the task – I lack
the qualifications. Certain it is that anyone who had strayed by
chance among those excellent people, lacking a doctorate or at the
absolute minimum a very good honours degree, would have felt
diffident and tongue-tied in the extreme; indeed even with these
recommendations, but lacking the easy fluency which knows how
to deploy difficult and complex, obscure and advanced ideas with
geniality and deceptive simplicity and unostentatious control,
such a person might have felt distinctly inferior and out of place.

The delightful atmosphere which I have just haltingly attempted
to convey was already well established when Dr Tuberose made
his entry. He was unaccompanied, embarrassingly so, for when
his wife had left him five months previously it had soon emerged
that she was living with a Chinese waiter in Burntisland. Cowperthwaite and Aminta, in fact, had invited him partly out of
sympathy and fellow-feeling, for Adrian, their seventeen year-old
son, was living with another Chinese waiter in Tollcross. When
Dr Tuberose came in they were all discussing Rudolf Steiner
play-groups. As Tuberose advanced into the room with an intent
but somehow abstracted look on his sensitive little face, a
knowing, almost scornful little smile playing about the corners of
his mouth, and an exalted expressiveness in his light grey eyes, the
guests turned towards him with genial, welcoming expansiveness.
Dr Tuberose nodded vaguely at his acquaintances, his eyes flickering over the company, searching for Pluckrose. At that moment,
an amazing incident occurred.

Demiurge, who up to that moment had been dozing comfort-

ably beside the fire, having decided that the conversation, fascinating though it doubtless was, was way above his head, now
suddenly sat up, the hair rising along his back, and staring at
Tuberose with every sign of venomous hostility, growled at him
in the most menacing manner, and even started to yap in a pitch
of hellish stridency, advancing towards Tuberose and then
backing away again as if uncertain whether the situation called for
attack or defence. Tuberose, quite unnerved, retreated against a
sideboard, and Cowperthwaite in complete consternation abandoned the drinks he had been pouring and hastened over, crying,
'Demmy! Demmy! What is it, darling? You know Uncle Marcus!
It's only Uncle Marcus, Demmy, he won't hurt you, sweetheart!'

Demiurge, however, was not to be pacified so easily. He was
now yapping furiously and pertinaciously, and as it were with a
growing confidence in the justice of his cause; Dr Tuberose had
retreated within a protective ring of guests, utterly taken aback
but conscious of a dawning recognition that something was afoot,
that there was more here than met the eye. Sterner measures were
clearly required, and now Cowperthwaite rapped out, 'Demiurge!'
in a tone of warning, and with a rising emphasis on the final
syllable.

The uttering of this shameful name had an instantaneous effect
on the poor animal. With an appearance of great fright he shot off
with his tail between his legs and slumped abjectly on the hearth-
rug; it was really impossible not to feel sorry for him. He now lay
unmoving with his head between his paws, and soon commenced
making ostentatious snuffling noises and settling his lips, as if he
had never had any other thought in his head but to prepare for
sleep. It was all a show, however. Shortly he began once more to
cast furtive glances at Dr Tuberose, and once the commotion had
died down a little and he was no longer an object of scrutiny, he
kept following 'Uncle Marcus' with his eyes, with an unfathomable gaze that spoke volumes, but in some unknown tongue.

The party had no sooner settled back into normality than the
telephone rang. Cowperthwaite left the room to answer it, and
after a brief absence returned and called over to Aminta, 'That
was Phil Pluckrose, sweetheart. He sends his apologies, they
won't be coming. It seems McSpale needed to see him very

urgently about something.' Dr Tuberose was at this moment in conversation with a psychiatrist whom he had always known simply as 'Justin's Daddy'. Justin's Daddy had a club foot, for which reason he had been called 'Dr Goebbels' at school, which just goes to show how cruel children can be; and a few unpleasant people still referred to him by that name, not of course in his hearing. Justin's Daddy, who had met Dr Tuberose socially on two or three previous occasions, had suddenly become interested in him when, a few minutes previously, he had overheard him say to Cowperthwaite, 'Did you notice how McSpale kept staring at me during the Department meeting? There was an awful depth and malignancy in his eye . . . ' ('Oh, dear,' Aminta had interrupted with sweet concern, 'has he got cancer?') Now, when the news about Pluckrose was announced, Dr Tuberose broke off in mid-sentence and his poetic face at once took on a horrified, haunted, harried look, a look which caused Justin's Daddy to observe him with an almost professional concern. But no one else noticed.

The company was artistically dispersed all round the room, chatting expansively. The subject of conversation was the reading given the previous Saturday evening by the poet Brechin of his epic work, 'The Old Dying Sheep'.

'I take it that it is intended as an allegory of the fate of the artist in a materialistic society', observed Robin Dross-Jones, who wrote a very highly regarded newpaper column, 'Vermicular Viewpoint'.

'Yes, but the symbolism can be understood at a number of different levels,' responded Cowperthwaite sagaciously. 'We could also, for instance, assume the old dying sheep to be Scotland.'

'And surely there's a rather impudent, tongue-in-cheek allusion to the motif of the young dying god?' suggested someone else.

'Indeed,' said Cowperthwaite, 'why not? The image means all of these things, of course, and at the same time none of them. Finally, perhaps, it's about himself that Brechin is speaking,' he closed, magisterially. There was a great deal of affirmatory grunting and vehement nodding of heads.

'Brechin was completely legless last time I saw him,' remarked Robin Dross-Jones.

'Legless?' cried Dr Tuberose suddenly, in terrible agitation. 'Did you say legless?'

The creator of 'Vermicular Viewpoint' stared at him. 'Yes, legless,' he replied. 'You know . . . drunk.'

'Ah,' said Dr Tuberose, relieved, but at the same time still suspicious.

'But that was after his mother's funeral, dear,' said Florrie Dross-Jones.

'My mother was always belittling me,' put in Dr Tuberose wildly, 'devaluing me, casting aspersions on me! "I'm sorry for your wife," she would say, "if you ever get one." I always remember that, I can never forget it! What a thing to say to a child: "I'm sorry for your wife, if you ever get one." '

'Oh, dear,' said Aminta, faintly.

'And now, you see,' continued Dr Tuberose relentlessly, 'she is living with a Chinese waiter in . . . in . . . Burntisland. Not that I have anything against the Chinese, who are an industrious little people. The man has legs, so far as I am aware, and not by accident. Yes, he has legs, and everything else that he needs to betray me!' He looked around the room and was vaguely aware of the terrible embarrassment and consternation which he was causing. 'I'm sorry,' he said, and passed his hand over his eyes. 'This is the price I have to pay for having the sensibility of a poet.'

No one said anything. After a quite long and very awkward silence, they all, as if by a prearranged signal, began talking about where they had been and what they were doing when Kennedy was assassinated.

'I was still at school,' said Aminta, and for some reason this was greeted with howls of urbane laughter. 'I can't remember what I was doing – I expect I was doing my sums.'

'I think I was cutting my toenails,' said Dr Tuberose. 'It's a strange thing, you know, but I have rather coarse feet. My hands are sensitive and artistic, but my feet are rather solid and coarse and peasant-like.'

Demiurge, who had been keeping his own counsel for some time, now growled most threateningly at Dr Tuberose. Cowperthwaite at once went over to the dog and tried to quieten him.

'Come on, Urgie-Purgie, who loves his daddy?' he coaxed gently.

But whoever loved his daddy, it didn't appear to be Urgie-Purgie. He sat up, staring at Dr Tuberose, and began once more to yap in a frightened but at the same time a challenging and even provocative tone. Dr Tuberose sprang to his feet in a dawning epiphany: he had just understood something. This was not Demiurge. This was not the Demiurge he knew, not the dog whose long floppy ears he had fondled when he was a puppy, no, no, no: this was, on the contrary, Philip Endymion Pluckrose, MA D Phil!

This insight did not represent quite such a remarkable imaginative leap on the part of Dr Tuberose as might at first appear. For, you see, he had already realised, quite suddenly that afternoon, that Pluckrose was the devil. The truth had dawned on him after it had struck him outside the lecture hall how Mephistophilean, even Luciferean, was Pluckrose's little black beard: it flashed on him then that he was not just metaphorically but literally in disguise, that he was in fact the devil! As he mulled over his dream of the previous night, it was quite clear to Dr Tuberose that the official in the form of a Himalayan bear whom McSpale had set on him could only be Pluckrose, that is, the devil, in another disguise. McSpale was God the Father, or more strictly (since Dr Tuberose was a man of sophisticated literary sensibility) he was a symbolic projection of God the Father; and he was testing Dr Tuberose by giving Satan power over him for a season, as he had done many years before with his servant Job. How perfectly it all fitted into place! How ever had he failed to see it before! He was being tested and proved like gold, and he must not be found wanting. And now Pluckrose the devil had come to him in yet another disguise, in the form of Demiurge the dog, and he must stand up to him and confront him boldly.

Dr Tuberose was now completely fearless. He advanced towards Demiurge with his left hand in his trouser pocket, a glass of wine in the other sensitive instrument, his head slightly on one side in an almost effeminate attitude, and a complacent, knowing smirk on his small, refined features.

'Do you imagine that I am stupid, Pluckrose?' he commenced

quietly, utterly in control of himself. The dog stopped yapping and stared in astonishment. 'Do you think you can fool *me*? You can appear as a dog or a Himalayan bear or as King-Kong, if you choose, it's entirely up to yourself. You are being used, Pluckrose, don't you realise that? You are no more than an instrument. Every dog has his day, and you have had yours. The future is mine. Justice will prevail, truth will prevail. You are yesterday's man, Pluckrose. In fact, if you only knew it, you were yesterday's man yesterday. I know who you are. But perhaps you don't know who McSpale is . . . I shall be Acting Head of the Department! It has been decided and ordained!'

Dr Tuberose's calm tone had been giving way during the course of this harangue to one of inspired, prophetic conviction, and now this in turn was converted into righteous fury. Dr Tuberose cast his glass to the floor, dropped to his knees and faced Demiurge nose to nose.

'Mongrel trash!' he cried impetuously. 'I'll cut off your legs, you mongrel trash! Dog of hell!'

Demiurge backed away from the raging madman, howling with terror. The ruin of a noble mind is always pitiful; but this was a terrible reversal to behold, the man in the role of the beast! But now the Cowperthwaites' twelve year-old daughter, who had been standing listening by the door, rushed forward fearlessly, gathered up Demiurge in her arms, and ran out with him, crying, 'Never mind, Demmy! Never mind, my poor little Semi-semi-demiurge! Pay no attention to the silly, bad man!'

Cowperthwaite had already gone into a huddle with Justin's Daddy; they were talking eagerly, excitedly but in hushed tones. Dr Tuberose found himself sitting bemusedly on a three-legged stool, in calm of mind, all passion spent; Florrie Dross-Jones had given him a Perrier water, which she said was very good for the digestion. Fragments of conversation reached Dr Tuberose from the group clustering around Justin's Daddy over by the door.

'I can arrange for him to be admitted tonight . . .'

'We'd better start phoning for a taxi right away, it'll take ages on a Friday night . . .'

'It's all right, we've ordered one already, you can take that, we can wait . . .'

'Poor man!'

'Phil Pluckrose'll have to take over his lecture course.'

'Out of the question with all his departmental responsibilities.'

'That's not till next year. Phil's the only one . . .'

'Oh, no, Angela Mulhearn could do it very competently. It's well within her field of interest.'

'Should we let Malitia know, do you think?'

'Good God, no!'

'Better phone his GP, perhaps. I think it's Gebbie.'

'No, no, there's no problem there, he can be taken in tonight.'

'No, no, I cannot be taken in!' cried Dr Tuberose suddenly. 'You can take me in, if you understand me, but I cannot be taken in. I know a hawk from a handsaw.'

'Don't worry, Marcus, Justin's Daddy is going to take you home; he'll give you something to make you sleep, you'll be fine in the morning!'

'I see, you want me to go with Dr Goebbels here? Well, that's all right! Legs eleven – bingo! And not by accident. Yes, the legs of a Chinese waiter, with a club foot at one end and betrayal at the other!'

'It's funny, you very seldom see a club foot nowadays,' said Aminta, in the general confusion quite forgetting about Justin's Daddy. Then she suddenly remembered! 'Oh, dear! But it's wonderful what they can do nowadays,' she added vaguely.

The door-bell rang. 'That's the taxi!' everbody shouted at once.

'I'll let the driver know you're coming,' said Robin Dross-Jones eagerly, and rushed down the stair.

Dr Goebbels took Dr Tuberose gently but very firmly by the elbow and steered him towards the front door; he let himself be taken, offering no resistance. Everyone was crowding around him with looks and words of sympathy and concern, but Dr Tuberose was no longer in need of sympathy or concern, for he had understood it all. Everything had suddenly become crystal-clear to him; and though it would be impossible to put into words the full depth and comprehensiveness of his understanding, there was no mistaking its reality, for his eyes glowed with exaltation, a smile of triumph played about his sensitive little mouth, and his whole being was suffused with a light of wonderful self-approbation.

At the head of the stair he turned and faced the assembled company once more, gazing at them as if from an immense height.

'I declare this meeting adjourned!' he cried with tremendous authority. 'As Acting Head of Department, I declare this meeting adjourned.'

Acquainted with Grief

Mr Stanley Kirkpatrick, a small, compact, rodent-like man in late middle age, clad in a long and loosely fitting tweed overcoat and an old-fashioned Homburg hat, stood busily in the vestibule of the public library. Even when doing nothing whatsoever, Mr Kirkpatrick contrived always to look busy. His eyes behind his thick horn-rimmed spectacles shone brightly, and one might say that he had the look of an inquisitive and somewhat complacent vole or dormouse. He had a sheaf of papers under an arm, and in his hand he clutched a pair of old leather gloves. He smiled away to himself, unobtrusively, a little nervously. He appeared to be waiting for someone or something, but he was not impatient: all would be well, he was sure of that.

Mr Kirkpatrick was a fire-loss adjuster, an elder of St Matthew's Parish Church, and a poet. He was, as a matter of fact, at the public library in order to attend a poetry reading and workshop, part of a local poetry festival, to be conducted by a small panel of poets of varying degrees of distinction, and the sheaf of papers under his arm represented an ample selection from his own poetic efforts. He had arrived, he believed, with a generous amount of time to spare, and was waiting in his self-effacing way for the appearance of some kent face, so that he might not enter the room in which the event was to be held in splendid isolation.

In reality, however, the workshop was already over. Mr Kirkpatrick had obtained his information from an out-of-date preliminary leaflet; since its publication, the event had been transferred from the afternoon to the morning. He believed that the workshop was to start at two o' clock, but it had actually been scheduled to end at one, though naturally it had overrun its time. Now, at about one thirty, most of the participants had already departed for the local hostelry. However, approaching the vestibule from the corridor were two poets whom Mr Kirkpatrick recognised, carrying bulging briefcases and accompanied by three acolytes. One of the poets was very fat and enormously tall, the other diminutive and meagre. Mr Kirkpatrick was not exactly acquainted with either of them, but he had been in their company. Tumbling to the situation instantly (though he could not account for his mistake), and covering his disappointment with practised aplomb, he scuttled towards them, full of good will.

'All over?' he observed cheerfully, without turning a hair. 'Went well, did it?'

The poets replied perfunctorily and passed on into the street, turning in the direction of the public house. Mr Kirkpatrick followed in their wake, falling in with the acolytes a little behind the impressively contrasting figures. The fat one, Brechin, carried his stomach before him as if to say, 'Fat is beautiful!' His girth was untidily stuffed into an old raincoat, so that he resembled a battered suitcase bundled full of old blankets which strove vainly to burst the protesting locks. Brechin had been reading extracts from his epic work 'The Old Dying Sheep', generally taken to be an allegory of the fate of the artist in a materialistic society, or perhaps of the condition of Scotland . . . many believed that the symbolism could be understood at a number of different levels.

The lean poet, Dunbar, was a busy engaging little chap, with curly hair and opinions on every subject – quite strong ones, too – and the ability to express them with most impressive fluency and assurance, so that never at all was he at a loss for words. Yet it is probable that if these fluid and suggestive sentences of Dunbar's were to be written down one after the other just as Dunbar said them, they would be seen to amount to nothing very much at all.

The bar was extraordinarily crowded, the group from the poetry workshop having more or less taken over the area nearest the door. The centre of attention was the poet McGarrigle, the most distinguished of the bards present, who, having during the workshop given the impression of submitting himself, probably out of a sense of compassion, to a boring and irksomely familiar routine, was now being witty in an abrasive but of course fundamentally kindly way.

As the latecomers stood around waiting to be served, Mr Kirkpatrick made a number of attempts to enter the conversation, but these met with extremely limited success until he offered to buy a round of drinks. Overjoyed by the sudden popularity which ensued, our amiable fire-loss adjuster made his way to the bar, and having with difficulty made his presence felt there, he bought a malt whisky for McGarrigle, a dram for Dunbar, and a nip and a pint for Brechin. Various hangers-on also added more modestly to the sum of his expenses, and Mr Kirkpatrick himself had a half-pint of cider. Almost immediately after they had received their drinks, however, the poets' interest in their benefactor showed signs of evaporating, and in no time at all they began to disperse in different directions. Mr Kirkpatrick, a shade puzzled, blinked a little but nonetheless continued to smile. He now found himself standing with a rather vivacious and not unattractive girl of about nineteen, who, having learned that he had missed the poetry workshop, thoughtfully began to tell him about everything that had happened there.

A married but childless man, Mr Kirkpatrick began to become extraordinarily confused. As he responded to the girl's story, keeping his eyes directed mainly to his shoes, his staccato questions and comments were punctuated by small, but strong, shrug-like convulsions of his shoulders, which soon involved the whole length of his arms and presently reached such a pitch that his sheaf of papers, which he still held grasped against his side by his elbow, became dislodged and scattered copiously about the floor. As he bent down to pick them up Mr Kirkpatrick for some reason suddenly started talking, and he continued to talk, rapidly and in low but insistent tones, as he dusted them off and stuffed them in an overcoat pocket. Indeed, there was no stopping him now: he was well and truly launched into an uninterruptable monologue.

He talked about the occasions on which he had previously met Dunbar and Brechin, about their qualities as poets, about the difficulties of small publishers and the state of poetry in Scotland. He talked about the problems he had in fitting time for poetry into his life, about his enthusiasm for poetry readings and workshops, about his struggle for recognition and the pains of rejection. When the girl, who was called Karen, managed to get to the bar to buy them another drink, he continued to talk at her over her shoulder, more insistently than ever. It seemed to her all at once, indeed, that an almost vatic tone had taken possession of his voice. The fact was, he had begun to declaim a poem.

Mr Kirkpatrick was now in the hands of a power stronger than himself. Though he had a sheet in his slightly trembling hand, he was reciting from memory; his voice had taken on a new confidence and authority, his eyes were shining brightly, his whole body seemed vibrant and expressive and he even gesticulated lightly at dramatic moments. He was still wearing his Homburg hat. The poem was speaking, in veiled but unmistakable language, of rejection, of rebuffs, of humiliations, but also of dedication and resilience and single-minded commitment. It spoke of a man alone, rejected of men and rejected of women, of sorrows and defeats, but it spoke too, and eloquently, of the unconquerable human spirit.

Those immediately around Mr Kirkpatrick had begun to listen, and soon their silence communicated itself to others further away. Even the poets turned towards him. Brechin gave the impression that he was observing the decencies, by an ostentatious act of self-control succeeding in not registering amusement, while Dunbar wore the somewhat astounded but eager look of one capable of making, and always ready to make, a seminar out of anything. For a moment, Mr Kirkpatrick had seized the attention of all, and silence reigned throughout the bar, comparatively speaking.

The poet now became aware, in one part of his mind, that he had an audience, and simultaneously he became conscious of the handicap imposed by his lack of inches. Truly to command his audience, he needed to be higher up, and it occurred to him that he ought perhaps to be standing on a chair. The idea was outrageous, he knew, but in spite of himself he half-paused in his delivery to look round for one. There was none to hand, however, and at once he thought better of his impulse and continued to declaim.

But the mistake had been made. Mr Kirkpatrick's flow had been interrupted and his self-consciousness had returned. His attention wandered, he stumbled in his declamation, the authority of his voice faltered. He could see that for his listeners the novelty of the happening had already worn off: some had begun to talk again, the poets were turning away. McGarrigle made a partly audible and none too complimentary remark. Moreover a small knot of educationally disadvantaged young persons, who had been playing darts at the far end of the bar, were showing every sign of becoming restive. Mr Kirkpatrick's moment had passed.

As it happened he was approaching the end of a section of his poem, and as he did so his voice trailed off into silence. Simultaneously, he realised that he had an extraordinary number of things to do. As he stuffed the sheet back in his pocket he was mumbling short, incomprehensible sentences, whether addressed to others or himself it was hard to say.

'That was marvellous!' said Karen kindly, 'Do you mean to say it's never been published?'

'Thank you . . . thank you . . . yes . . . no . . . great many things to do, must be going . . . great many things to do . . . thank you . . .'

Mr Kirkpatrick raised his hat to Karen, turned and darted out of the bar. In the street he hesitated as if uncertain in which direction to turn, started off left then wheeled round in full stride and set off right. He scuttled along rapidly with his eyes on the ground, keeping close to the wall, resembling a small wounded animal attempting to remain invisible while escaping from a predator. One would almost have thought that he was limping.

Original Sin

I

Full-length on his stomach in the ditch-like depression, his chin resting among the coarse grass on its verge, fingers dug deep into moss, soft muddy dampness beneath his thighs, peering through the tufts of heather; almost panting as he strove to hear, panic at his heart. The group of figures moving to and fro among the pine trees two hundred yards ahead of him, the reservoir lying leaden beyond them under the dull sky, the voices mostly muffled but every now and again rising sharply for an instant only to fall again before he could distinguish the words. Then 'Here!' came a sudden shout from a poking, prodding shape in a donkey jacket, and again, sharp with rising excitement, 'here!' His breath was halted with horror in his throat and he gripped compulsively at the tufts of grass. From all directions the dark figures came hurrying to where the man who had shouted had been digging. The latter held something up for all to see, and while some jostled up to gaze at it others fell to scrabbling with frenzied energy around the spot where it had been found. Very soon a new, loud and concerted shout arose and at once a further find was held up to view. This time he could make it out clearly from where he lay watching, an elongated stick-like thing showing up pale in the mirkiness of the pine wood – a bone, a long thin pale bone, and, as he knew all too well, a human bone. He moaned. The helpless terror of discovery was upon him and his brain and his body were numbed. He struggled to rise from the pit in which he lay, to rise and flee into the enveloping dusk, but his limbs failed him, his arms had no strength in them and they could not raise him up . . .

He was awake. He opened his eyes in the dim light of dawn, and lay on in the irremediable sickness of his soul. He knew that he had dreamed, that the discovery had not taken place, but the full horror and foulness of his deed overwhelmed his spirit. How had he ever forgotten it? How was that possible? How could he have lived with this act for all those years, repressed it and erased it so successfully that his waking life had not known of it at all? How had he walked about on the face of the earth with this weight inside him, how had he moved among people, how had he laughed and worked and eaten and loved? When all along, deep within him, he had known?

He moaned aloud and tried to move. He was nearly off the edge of the bed, his right arm was dead. He became aware of his immediate situation. The woman he loved lay beside him, turned away from him, he could feel her back against his front, feel the silkiness of her buttocks against his belly, make out the contour of her body and the darkness of her head on the pillow. His dead right arm was pinioned under her neck. He tried to concentrate, and a thin flash of hope illuminated his consciousness. This deed, had he dreamt that too? No, no, he had not dreamt that: the illumination receded into dimness and despair flooded his mind. Think, think, it was necessary to think. Yes, but yes, that idea wanted to re-establish itself, to assert its plausibility. It wanted to lie to him, to perpetuate that old lie, to whisper to him that he had never killed. He tried to move the fingers of his dead hand but he could feel nothing, it was as if his arm had been cut off below the shoulder. Back and forth went these ideas in his mind: it's true, it isn't true, it's true, it isn't true. After about five minutes he was finally sure. No, it was not true. He had never killed anyone in his life.

He sighed with weakness and weariness. He endeavoured to raise himself but could not get a purchase: he had almost been pushed out of his own bed, the woman lay solidly in the middle and he was half hanging over the edge. He began to try to pull his arm out from under her; it was not easy. She stirred and made a noise in her throat. He cursed and pulled again. At once she moaned and half turned over on her back, covering more of his arm. As she did so she tossed her head from side to side on the pillow: 'No,' she said, 'no!' 'Sorry,' he replied, but she sighed and was still. He tried again and she whimpered. He peered into her face and saw that she was asleep, but that her brows were pulled together in a look of distress. He was moved and felt an access of love for her, and with it a thin tugging of desire. He held his breath and pulled his arm out sharply from under her; this time she did not stir.

Carefully he climbed out of bed and walked over to the window, moving his arm about to get the circulation going. He drew the curtain back further and looked out over the neighbouring gardens; it was quite light but the sun was not yet up and there was a dampness in the air. He felt chilled. He was greatly relieved now in the knowledge that what he had dreamt had no solid reality, yet somehow not so relieved as he ought to have been: a nasty taste remained in the mouth of his spirit. He had a powerful impression that he had experienced that crushing sense of guilt before. When ... when? The memory was not too far away, there was some connection with his standing here at the window, looking down into the garden ...

He had it. He was four years old. His parents had taken him on a visit to some friends. He remembered a large house surrounded by a beautiful garden, away out somewhere on the edge of town. Two boys, much older than himself, and a girl, only a little older. There was something funny about the girl: although she was older than him she did not seem to be able to talk properly. She kept pointing to him and saying 'Bibby'. He felt somehow insulted and wanted to protest in some way, but he did not know how to set about it. He looked at the boys as if for guidance, but they seemed to be very tolerant of the girl and unaware of his distress and embarrassment.

The next thing he remembered he was out in the garden with the girl at the back of the house. The boys had disappeared. They were supposed to be playing but he was feeling very useless and unhappy. He could not make the girl understand anything he said or do anything sensible at all, she just kept running aimlessly to and fro and shouting. She looked very odd and his already fastidious nature shrank from her in fear and disgust. Suddenly she stopped running about, stood still and pointed at him. 'Bibby!' she cried, 'Bibby!' Rage sprang up in him. A long clothes pole lay on the thick grass. He made for it and began to pick it up. He wanted to annihilate the girl. He was going to hit her on

the head with the pole and if possible kill her. 'Bibby!' she shouted
again. He struggled to raise the pole; it was very heavy, but he had
it round the middle. Just at that moment he heard his mother's
voice calling – he did not take in the words. Guilt flashed in his
heart. He let go of the pole as if it had been red-hot and looked
up: his mother and the mother of the girl were standing looking
down at them from an upstairs window. They were both smiling
and he could not understand why: he stood before them exposed
and naked, caught in the act, his face on fire. The two mothers
seemed to be pretending not to know what he intended, but he
knew that it could only be an act to save embarrassment all
round, for his guilt was everywhere about him; unhidden, he
was certain, from those smiling eyes. Yes, this shame and terror
of exposure was the very feeling of his dream: what he had
purposed secretly and in safety, in the private places of his heart,
was openly known.

II

The terror, the terror: nights of long darkness and encroaching
cold, the short bitter days. We sit in front of the log fire, the two
of us, crouching towards its crackling heat. Heaping on more fuel,
inadvertently I move one of the logs so that it is not burning
properly, and the other is angry. As I try to shove it back into
place it seems to move of its own accord, what seems like an eye
appears and then a rudimentary ear. 'My God,' I cry, 'that log's
alive!' No surprise to him, though; he savagely pokes the fire
while the log twists and moans. He has always known that logs
can live, and this one he means to kill. I see now what it is, this
log, it is the head and neck of a horse which writhes in agony!
Somehow it tells its story – how it was cut down by human cruelty
and taken from its home.

Things are different now: a plastic surgeon has been at work.
This former log, this erstwhile horse, he has converted it into
human form, the incisive one, recreated it in his own image; the

image of a repulsively handsome and decadent young man, an actor who struts forth his arrogance upon the stage. He holds the log in subjection as his servant (oh yes, you can still tell, from certain lumps and scars about the forehead, that this was once a log). The log is murderously resentful: a fight to the death will break out between these twins.

III

The baby lies there, looking up and smiling, a plump and happy baby with nothing but love in its heart. In the shaded room the people pass in and out, looking at the baby and admiring it, making friendly noises, sometimes leaning down and chucking it under the chin. The baby responds delightedly, it coos and gurgles with joy.

It is the dark man's turn: his form overshadows the cot, he gazes down into the baby's eyes, smiling, his purpose complete within him. He smiles to let the others know his good intent, he smiles at the baby to establish as it were a conspiracy between them; the shame of his perfidy gnaws him like a worm. Yes, the baby knows all right, but will it betray him? Will it remember, and will it forgive him? He gently fondles the infinitely soft and delicate skin beneath the baby's chin, all the time smiling his gentle love . . . But the baby's smile is less certain now, a cloud passes over, at any moment it may cry. At once, gritting his teeth, he digs the nails of his thumb and forefinger deep within that unresisting flesh.

IV

Crawl, crawl on, lump. On your belly, arms pinioned at the sides, snaking onwards, gasping and panting. Tighter and tighter.

Through the tortuous passageways of this castle. Is there space in the distance? Is there breath? On, then, tighter and tighter, wriggling and squirming. This creeping thing, going on its belly. This slimy squirming thing, eating dust. This tiny piece of contemptible obscene matter, this living bird-dropping. I. Crush it beneath the heel.

Fates

To be lying on a pavement on a raw November evening, severely injured in a road accident caused by a moment's inattention, partially covered by the overcoats of passers-by, surrounded by inquisitive rush-hour crowds, waiting interminably for the ambulance.

To be shut inside a derelict shower-cubicle in an abandoned hotel in Macedonia, with no handle on the inside of the door, in the darkness, in the silence, in the thick acrid air, on the nineteenth of August, utterly beyond the range of any human ear.

To be running away from a mad dog, still two hundred yards from the safety of a shop doorway, over rough cobbles, wearing clogs, suffering from gout, sciatica and bronchial congestion, and knowing that you're not going to make it.

To be falling, finally, down the outside steps of the Eiffel Tower, in conspicuous summer clothes, with a heavy dinner on the belly, and no head for heights.

Yes, there are assuredly many worse fates than to love without hope.

The Emperor Bolingbroke III

The Emperor Bolingbroke III lay gasping and peching on a divan, half propped-up upon a mound of silken cushions, gorged with sticky buns. At his right side, holding one of his pudgy hands, knelt an almond-eyed concubine, who from time to time dabbed at his brow with a kerchief of muslin, moistened with eau-de-cologne; while behind him towered two gross eunuchs, to whom it fell to keep the torpid air in circulation with fans and fly-swats, driving off with shrill curses the mosquitoes, humming-birds and giant butterflies which ever and anon sought to alight upon the potentate's glistening pate.

'See's a big Newcastle an' a packet o' salted peanuts, hen,' begged the suffering monarch, who since his elevation to the imperial dignity five years previously had retained an unspoilt enthusiasm for the simple things of life. Alerted by his physician to the dangers of a gut-distending surfeit, he had earlier that day been obliged to make a bitter and corrosive choice between strawberry cheese-cake and cherry meringue pie; the deprivation had left him demoralised, dispirited and over-anxious, a prey to nervous hallucinations and morbid suspicions. As his tawny-hued paramour, a young cheetah on a silver chain attached to an amethyst-encrusted collar padding at her heel, now withdrew to fetch his requirements, the Emperor slumped back upon his cushions, sucking his thumb, his mind invaded by a spiritless depression.

But now the soporific torpor of the sultry afternoon was disturbed by the precipitate entry of a wretched, ill-clad, famine-reduced figure who scuttled past the astounded major-domo, threw himself face down at a run upon the tesselated marble floor and by the impetus of his own propulsion slid on his stomach the remaining fifteen yards to the foot of the Emperor Bolingbroke's couch, where after lavishing kisses without restraint upon the plump and grimy toes which protruded from among the damask draperies, he delivered himself of the obsequious harangue which follows.

'O happiest and most fortunate of mortals' (he commenced), 'destined by the ineluctable decree of a sagacious heaven to everlasting dominion over the fowls of the deep and the beasts of the upper ether, it is the unctuous petition of this humblest and least worthy of your subjects that Your Honour's illustrious eye may alight with grudging favour upon the tasteless effusions of your obedient servant's servile pen. That Your Honour may long live to display your distinguished virtues and to enjoy in the favours and attentions of your amiable courtesans the just rewards of such patronising condescension, is the ardent desire . . .'

'You takin' the piss?' interrupted the touchy potentate, raising himself puffing and blowing on one elbow, his shifty little eyes restless with suspicion. Immediately upon his words the flabby but generously proportioned emasculate stepped forward and fell to chastising the feeble and prostrate youth with fly-whisks and feather-dusters, raising noxious odours from his vermin-infested rags. Moths, spiders and field-mice now detached themselves from his howling person and fled before the onslaught of the *castrati*; shortly little shrieks of femine terror spoke distantly of their advent among the recesses of the imperial harem.

When at last the emasculated giants ceased from their exertions, leaving the intruder a gently palpitating heap of rags upon the tiles, they collapsed panting and sweating on two stools by the doorway, abandoning their master to the unwelcome attentions of airborne nuisances, which he vainly attempted to ward off with ineffectual flappings of his arms. At this juncture his dark-skinned doxy returned to the audience chamber, bearing upon a silver salver a packet of salted peanuts and a pint of Guinness. The Emperor's mouth dropped open a little, an expression of vague, half-resentful bewilderment flitted momently across his countenance, and finally a peevish outrge could be observed battling with despair for the mastery of his features. He groaned.

'Aw, fur Chrissake! I asked fur a big Newcastle an' ye've brought me a fuckin' Guinness!'

The Tweak

There are some who would have it that the matter of the tweak was nothing but an 'insignificant incident', and one moreover which ought not to be dignified by examination; and from the point of view of anyone not inward with it, such an estimate would be justified. Yet, can an 'insignificant incident' which is remembered with bitterness ten years after the event, and not only is remembered but remains so fraught with emotional resonance that the mere mention of it is enough to reduce grown men to tears – can such an incident really be as trivial as a superficial appraisal might suggest? There are many question-marks hanging over the whole episode, and numerous details are not clear to this day and seem destined to remain shrouded in mystery.

That Hilda tweaked Louisa's nose seems certain, though there are in fact many who would dispute even that, Hilda not least among them. Actually, the only unexceptionable facts are that Louisa claimed that her nose had been tweaked by Hilda, and that Hilda denied it, and although the thing happened in full view of at least a dozen people it is impossible to go further than that or to obtain definite corroboration either way. One version I have heard is that as Hilda passed Louisa on her way to the toilet Louisa deliberately blew smoke in her face, and that Hilda simply raised her hand to wave the smoke away from her eyes, an action which from certain angles could be very open to misinterpretation as the tweaking of Louisa's nose. Others maintained that Hilda did indeed touch the organ, but only to flick away a speck of cigarette ash which by ill chance had alighted on the tip. But an opposing, and articulate, school of thought has it that she did in fact tweak it, and very hard indeed, and actually drew blood; though whether this action was retaliatory or unprovoked again gives rise to dissension.

It is perhaps unlikely after such a lapse of time that we shall ever now be able to sift out all this conflicting evidence and establish the truth of the matter – whatever 'the truth' may be. What interests me more than any mere facts, however, is the play of emotional forces which gave rise alike to the happening and to the various interpretations to which it has been subjected. For undoubtedly the tweak (or indeed the alleged tweak – it doesn't matter in this context) cannot be considered a fortuitous event: one way or the other, it had been a long time in the making, all the more so because its evolution had been subterranean. There are those who claim that Hilda came to the party firmly intending to tweak Louisa's nose, and it is not impossible; but neither is it impossible that Louisa invited and desired it, perhaps even asked Hilda to her party with the express objective – I don't say of having her nose tweaked, specifically, but at any rate of provoking or conjuring up an incident which would show Hilda up in a bad light. If that is true, and I don't say it is, she certainly was not aware of it, not at any rate until her objective was in the process of consummation. Such little dramas take on a life of their own, they make us their slaves or puppets, the play becomes the thing, to such an extent in fact that it is perfectly possible for honest and intelligent people, not to speak of others, to have a firm and unshakeable conviction that events took place which did not, or that events did not take place which did, especially when sex is involved. And that sex was involved in this particular little drama there is scarcely any room for doubt.

For the plain truth of the matter is that both Hilda and Louisa were in love with McGarrigle, one of our local geniuses. Hilda had, in fact, until a short time before the incident of the tweak, been his mistress, while Louisa was perhaps the front runner among those aspiring to succeed her in that role. I must explain here that McGarrigle, although an ill-favoured and repulsively overweight little man, had apparently in some abundance that indefinable but undeniably advantageous quality known as 'charisma'. If it wasn't his 'charisma' that was responsible for his success with women, then it can only have been his 'creativity'.

McGarrigle was employed at that time as a short-order cook in a mediocre Italian restaurant, and even in this sphere he was recognised by his employers as being 'creative' or at least as bringing a 'creative attitude' to bear on his work. Some would have it that his creativity began and ended with the striking of attitudes, but that is not really fair. He was in fact responsible for several immensely long dramatic monologues and a one-act play about the love of the poet Keats for Fanny Brawne, which I am told went over very well when a local drama group performed it on the Edinburgh Festival Fringe one year. What probably counted for more however was the air he had of studied arrogance, an arrogance which was not all the same especially designed to direct attention to his works, and may as a matter of fact have been designed to draw it away from them, the adoption of such a pose intendedly sufficing in itself as a proof of extraordinary talent.

The episode of the tweak, though perhaps the most inwardly revealing, was by no means the most dramatic example of the passions which could be aroused by McGarrigle's creativity and charisma. The most dramatic is represented by the events that occurred on the occasion of his famous poetry reading at our local ice rink a few years ago. Upwards of four thousand people had paid sums of up to £65 on the black market for tickets for this memorable event, in which McGarrigle had been billed by the promoters as undertaking to read, with suitable pauses for refreshment and sustenance, for a full week. On the evening of the fifth day, however, McGarrigle announced blandly and with only the most perfunctory apologies that he was tired and would be concluding his reading at the end of that night's session, in only two and a half hours' time. The most astonishing uproar ensued, and almost at once a shot rang out from one of the side balconies. I should explain at this point that McGarrigle had gathered his unruly locks together in a pony-tail lest they should obscure his vision while he was reading and impede his tempestuous flow. The bullet so impetuously fired by some distraught fan now severed the elastic band securing this appendage and released in a sudden dazzling torrent that golden cascade. Pandemonium at once broke out, and in spite of the tight security measures in force and the desperate efforts of the poet's bodyguard two young girls succeeded in clambering onto the stage and grabbing hold of the strands of the erstwhile pony-tail, with which they proceeded to stage a kind of macabre tug-of-war, pulling frantically in opposite directions as each endeavoured to gain possession of the person of the luckless poet. McGarrigle was magnificent. Completely ignoring the disturbance, and truly *au-dessus de la mêlée*, he continued to read imperturbably, and in clear and ringing tones, even while being dragged from one side of the stage to the other by the screaming harpies, and with his hair coming away in chunks. Indeed I am told that he has never read better.

I digress, however. To return at last to the tweak, I see it – and this is what I've been leading up to all along – as a kind of epiphany, a 'sudden spiritual manifestation' as Joyce would have it, bodying forth the very essence of what McGarrigle means to suffering humanity today. As such it will some day, I believe, provide the starting-point for one of his greatest works; if, that is, McGarrigle ever writes any great works. And if he doesn't, it will only go to show what an extraordinary fuss people will sometimes make about absolutely nothing at all.

Dealing with a Bore

I seem to be a person who is exceptionally vulnerable to the attentions of bores. I am not a conversationalist, you see, perhaps because I feel that fundamentally there is nothing much in life that is worth talking about, or at least that talking never really did much in the way of good to anybody or anything. Having so little to say for myself, in order to give the impression that in spite of that I am contributing to a conversation by my interest, intelligence and observation – in short, by being a good listener – I try to maintain an observant, intelligent and interested look on my face when someone is talking to me; and where bores are concerned, that's fatal.

Let me say at once, in case the feeling should suggest itself that I am in any way hard-hearted, that I'm far from being unsympathetic to bores. According to a psychological theory I read about recently, bores were never listened to as children, so that they are condemned for the rest of their lives to go on trying to gain their parents' attention, an ambition in which they can never now be successful; and that is of course a very sad thing. That granted, however, the fact remains that you have to look after yourself in this life, otherwise you're sunk.

Accordingly it is more or less essential to have contingency plans up your sleeve if you mix much with bores. Unfortunately the resourcefulness of bores, and their immunity to the promptings of conscience, are generally such as to confound the best-laid schemes. You may fondly suppose for instance that you can get off with passing the time of day with a bore, and if it's a sunny one and your mood full of the milk of human kindness you can even be betrayed in the first few seconds into imagining that he's really not too bad, and agreeing to join him for a half pint. In no time at all he'll have you pinioned in a corner, he'll overbear you and stand up close to you, probably spit into your drink, and then simply talk you into the ground. Moreover, he'll notice at once if you're contemplating flight, he will recognise your intention in the very first flicker of the eyes in the direction of the door, and from that moment will keep up such an unremitting and pertinacious verbal assault that you can escape him only by resorting to unconscionable rudeness. In effect, he's challenging you to tell him that he's a bore, and counting on your good nature that you won't; or failing your good nature, on your sense of social propriety. Some bores will actually go so far as to ask if they're boring you, or more often beg for reassurance that they're not; and then they appear very hurt, and in a self-righteous kind of way too, if you tell them the truth.

There is one bore in particular of my acquaintance whom I'd like to tell you about. I've known him in a vague sort of way for several years, and we have a common interest in early Celtic history. This unfortunate man often has most interesting information to impart on this fascinating topic, and though he must long ago have recognised that he bores me stiff he can't for the life of him make out why. (He just cannot understand that it is not his subject-matter that is boring, but his insistence.) He launches into the most extraordinary speeches the moment he meets me, and expects an intelligent response too, so that he can be reassured as to how interesting he is. Usually I retreat before him inch by inch, and inch by inch he advances until he has me flattened against a car door, or perhaps a set of railings. The more it is borne in upon him that he is boring me and that I am desperate to get away, the more relentlessly and determinedly does he strive to be interesting, to hold my attention. 'This *must* interest him!' I can almost hear him think. He admitted to me once, in a confidential or unguarded moment, that he had been snubbed and rejected all his life, and he genuinely had not the least idea why.

One day I saw him bearing down on me in the street, a well-heeled sprightly middle-aged bore with brief-case and umbrella. There was no possibility of escape. With scarcely a 'How are you?' he at once began to recount to me in minute detail the contents of a recently published learned paper which seemed to provide new evidence in support of O'Rahilly's long-discredited theory that Ireland had been colonised by P-Celtic tribes before the Gaels. Everything he was telling me was really quite indescribably interesting, there is no doubt of that, and yet within seconds I was in a state of blind panic, frantically in search of any tiniest chink in the armour of his discourse which might admit the blade of my 'Well, I'm afraid I'm in a bit of a hurry . . '. But here my innate decency let me down time and again. I obviously should have stuck my oar in decisively the very first instant he drew breath, but I felt that in politeness a slight pause was called for; it need really be only a minuscule gesture but some token pause there had to be. Of course I should have known from experience that this bore would be quite merciless towards such weakness. The hesitation of a fraction of a second, my mouth already open to form the saving words, the very sound rising in the throat – too late, he was off again. This occurred three or four times before I finally lost my head. When that happened, though, I didn't even bother to wait for the next drawing of the bore's breath, but gasped 'I'm going in here' while he was absolutely in full flight, and turned and fled up the steps of the nearest building, which turned out to be a university department of Estate Management. Casting a furtive glance back from within the safety of the doorway I saw him already scuttling away in the opposite direction as fast as his legs could carry him, like a wounded rabbit.

Bores are creatures of remarkable resilience, however, and hope springs eternal in their all-too-human breasts. Only a few days ago I had just stepped into a lift in a local government building and the doors were already closing when I saw the bore leaping eagerly towards me across the vestibule, waving his umbrella. I could easily have let events take their course without incurring reproach, but some masochistic or perhaps sadistic impulse made me jam my foot between the doors and then bang the 'Open Door' button with my fist. There was no one else in the lift. The bore trotted up; I didn't let him in, however, discouraging his entry partly with my outstretched right hand which I kept pressed on the button, partly by placing my left arm akimbo on my hip. The bore was much more intent on talking than on entering the lift, anyway, and immediately launched forth. I felt an immense sense of power at that moment. For the first time in my experience I was not at his mercy, but he at mine. All I had to do to finish him off was to remove my hand from the 'Open Door' button; and moreover that was such a negative action, something really so much in the natural and inevitable way of things, that it couldn't possibly be thought of as in any way an offensive or spiteful act. The lift was needed elsewhere, after all, already it was beginning to buzz impatiently as it received summonses from above, and besides the bore might not even have wanted to go up. I let him ramble on for perhaps fifteen seconds, then at the words 'this remarkable new find of a coin of Vercingetorix', I released the button with a helpless shrug of the shoulders which dissembled a malicious joy. Pride goes before a fall, however. As he saw what was happening the bore bounded forward with a lightning reflex born of despair, and succeeded in thrusting his umbrella into the gap. For an agonising half-second the doors seemed to hesitate, then with weary resignation they reopened, admitting the trium-phant bore. I pressed the button for my floor and up we went, the bore of course rattling away ninety to the dozen. But I had an appointment upstairs and the trial, I thought, would not be long. Then all at once the lights flickered, the lift seemed to be moving with less confidence, less decisiveness; there came a slight judder, then a second more distinct, and it had come to a halt, between the eighth and ninth floors. Resigning myself to my fate, I turned my face to the wall. Only an hour before I had read in my morning paper that all the lift-repair men in the city would be on strike that week.

Herdman's Chiropractic Diary

Oct. 23rd

The place: an American city. Today I pay my first visit to the chiropractor to whom I've been recommended. My complaint: a partially numb left arm and hand, of three months' duration, accompanied by muscular heaviness. The receptionist tells me that the chiropractor has been called away on an emergency, but if I wish I can see his junior partner, Dr Klack. If however I see Dr Klack today he will continue to treat me. I agree. I wait for half an hour before being called into Dr Klack's room. He is a tall, lean, bespectacled man approaching forty, with fair greying hair brushed forwards to dissimulate his baldness. He greets me cheerily, looking me honestly in the eye. As I recount my symptoms he regards me with a friendly, stupid, quizzical look, similar to that which a ventriloquist directs at his dummy when attempting to divert attention from the movements of his own mouth. He examines me, pulling limbs back and forth, testing muscular responses, prodding here and there. I am quite impressed. As I lie on the couch my eyes flit around the room and I see that it is liberally adorned with coloured photographs of a grossly overweight young Indian whom I recognise as the Guru Maharaj Ji, head of the Divine Light Mission. I remember him from posters bearing his image which appeared on hoardings in Edinburgh some years ago, singing the praises of the 'fifteen year-old Perfect Master'. Most of these posters had quickly acquired balloons issuing from the mouth of the Perfect Master and attributing to him such confessions as 'I am a fat slob' and 'I am a perfect bastard.'

Dr Klack decides that an X-ray examination would be advantageous. I am ushered into the X-ray room where I wait for fifteen minutes, then moved with apologies into a third room where I wait a further half hour. Eventually Dr Klack reappears and takes the necessary pictures. I note with satisfaction, from the cyclostyled information handout given me by the receptionist, that Dr Klack has received at chiropractic college 292 class hours of instruction in X-ray, as compared to the forty-eight hours received by a graduate of John Hopkins Medical School. This examination completes the day's proceedings.

Oct. 24th

The X-rays have been developed. Dr Klack invites me to take a seat. He looks moderately grave, but honest, direct, and, above all, in control. I find myself adopting the air of eager, co-operative but slightly apprehensive attentiveness which his mien seems to call for. He shows me the X-rays, copiously marked with red lines, angles and calculations. My spine, as I will observe, deviates from the straight and narrow in several places. My neck has suffered an 85% loss of curve. 'But the most prominent feature of these plates,' says Dr Klack, 'is this.' He taps with his ballpoint an ominous bulge somewhere among my ribs, and his business-like gravity is a little more marked. 'That's calcification on the aorta. If we don't do something about that you're gonna have real problems in the years ahead. Big problems.' He nods his head. 'But we're gonna get you back into shape.' I heave a little sigh of relief: I really can't help it. Dr Klack questions me about diet, exercise and so on. Right enough, I scarcely touch vegetables; do eat a lot of fruit, though. Don't go in for any sporting activities, but then I do walk a lot ... Dr Klack looks kindly at me. 'You seem pretty tense.' God, Klack, who wouldn't be? 'We're gonna have to put some dietary supplements into you. Make up for the way you've been eating over all these years. Do you ever meditate, John?' I shake my head, uncomfortably aware of the cunning little eyes of the Perfect Master gazing down at me, bright beads in an expanse of jelly-fish. 'I have thought about it from time to time.' 'Do you a lot of good.' He gives me a long, thoughtful look, nodding decisively. 'I'll show you what I propose that we do for you here.' Klack now produces a cyclostyled sheet with a few blank spaces filled in in red ink, which is however headed 'Confidential Report of Chiropractic Examination and Recommendations prepared in detail especially for Mr John M. Herdman.' The recommendations in my case are for twenty-one initial visits over a period of seven weeks, to include, apart from regular spinal adjustments, twelve sessions of traction, twelve of deep sound treatment, meridian therapy and graph, and Biochemical analysis. I agree, of course. The cost, to include free comparative X-rays if paid for in advance, will be a round $400.

Oct. 27th

My first adjustments go smoothly and I continue to be impressed by Dr Klack. I also spend six minutes in traction, my neck stretched in a harness as I lie tensely on my back on the couch trying to avoid looking at the Perfect Master. The thought occurs to me that it might be dangerous to sneeze while in traction, and after I am released I ask Dr Klack what would happen if I did. Dr Klack takes it as a joke. 'Don't do that!' he snorts. 'Don't ever sneeze while you're in that contraption! I really do not advise that at all!' After that I don't dare ask him, as I had intended, what would happen in the event of an earthquake.

Next he asks me to look at him, and stares dreamily into my eyes. 'You've got a big circulatory problem,' he says. 'I can see it in your eyes. Do you know that white circle you've got around your iris? That's an arcus senilis.' He peers into my eyes with a torch. 'And there's definite cerebral anaemia, with evidence of thyroid involvement. We're gonna have to get that blood flowing more briskly through your brain. I want you to brush your whole body with a stiff bristle brush twice daily. I also want you to lie on wooden slabs for a half an hour each day with your head six inches lower than your feet. You can do that after the exercises I'm gonna show you right now. And next week we'll put some deep sound into you, that'll really get the circulation going. Balance your meridians, too.'

Oct. 30th

I am beginning to get a little suspicious of Dr Klack. I find it somewhat surprising that not one of the many physicians and specialists I have seen over years of hypochondria has ever told me that I had any circulatory or arterial problem. And I definitely remember being told that the arcus senilis has absolutely no known clinical significance. Also my arm doesn't feel any better. Still, it's early days yet.

Today I have my meridians balanced. I hold onto a metal rod while Dr Klack prods the ends of my fingers and toes with an instrument rather like the tape head demagnetiser I have for my music centre. When he prods, a little pointer on a gauge attached to his machine indicates the levels of vital energy emanating from various organs. My meridians are pretty well balanced, he says, except that there's an indication of a lack of energy from my kidneys. To put this right he stabs rapidly away at a certain point on my little toe with another instrument resembling a ballpoint pen, only much sharper. This is rather painful. Subsequent testing confirms that the energy has risen to its correct level. I am once more impressed. 'That's part of your problem dealt with,' says Dr Klack efficiently.

While he goes to attend to another patient, the doctor's receptionist administers deep sound. This is done by pressing an electrical contraption on each side of my neck for several minutes. 'It's fantastic stuff, this,' the girl tells me. 'I sure hope it does as much for you as it did for me.' I say I hope so too.

Nov. 1st

Feeling no better. Today I undergo my Biochemical analysis. I do so lying on my stomach, so I am not quite sure exactly what is going on. 'We do this analysis via the energy field surrounding the area of your legs,' explains Klack. He has with him his receptionist, who is in charge of a tray of samples of vitamin pills. Klack takes hold of my feet and pushes and pulls my legs, while I feel something cool placed on the small of my back. This process determines with quite extraordinary rapidity exactly what vitamin supplements I stand in need of, and even what commercial formula suits me best. 'You're real big on Vitamin B,' observes Klack. 'You mean I need a lot of it?' I ask uncertainly. 'You sure as hell do,' he replies chirpily. 'Gonna get you back into shape with these supplements. We'll have them ready for you next week.'

Nov. 3rd

Klack full of bonhomie. 'How's he doing today?' he almost shouts as he comes in to release me from the traction harness. I tell him that my arm always seems worse after a session of the exercises he's recommended. 'Show me how you're doing that cervical extension exercise,' he demands. I demonstrate, convinced that I have followed the directions on his instruction sheet implicitly and religiously. 'You're doing it all wrong,' says Klack sternly. 'This is how you should do it.' He performs the exercise, so far as I can tell, exactly as I did it. 'There. You were doing it wrong. That's why you've got a sore neck. I'd have a sore neck too if I did what you've been doing.' (I don't, of course, have a sore neck at all.) Klack now twists his neck into a grotesque posture not remotely like anything I have done. 'Wow! That hurts!' he exclaims with a broad and genial grin. 'Follow the instructions. These exercises are specific.'

Before I leave he brings in a large bag containing half a dozen bottles of vitamin pills of every sex, colour and creed. These are my supplies for three weeks, amounting to twenty-six pills every day. The cost is $40.

Nov. 15th

After three weeks, three days a week, of spinal adjustments, traction and deep sound, plus Biochemical analysis, meridian therapy and dietary supplements, my arm is certainly no better, and on the whole perhaps actually a little worse. I make this point to Klack, as hesitantly and reasonably and at the same time as persuasively as possible. I can tell that he is put out, but he responds with dignity. 'I can appreciate your concern,' he concedes. 'But this is natural healing, and natural healing takes time. We don't use knives or drugs in this treatment. If I cut you open with a knife I could probably cure you in no time. But that wouldn't be so good, would it now?' I shake my head. How can I disagree?

Nov. 27th

Over the weekend I have read some rather startling allegations in the local newspaper. Following mass suicides among religious fanatics at Jonestown, Guyana, and subsequent hysteria over cults, two former aides of the Guru Maharaj Ji have denounced him as a hypocrite and sadist. If these allegations are to be trusted, the Perfect Master smokes, drinks and takes drugs, all of which are expressly forbidden by his teaching, spends most of his time watching television, is subject to violent temper tantrums, and has the unpleasant habit of pouring corrosive chemicals over his disciples and kneeing them in the groin. I am most eager to find out how Klack has reacted to these revelations. Will the photographs have been removed as deleterious to business, or will he be anxious to demonstrate his loyalty, at least until the charges have been either proved or discredited? When I reach his office it becomes clear that he is going to brazen it out. The Guru is still very much in evidence, his simpering and fetid little smile impervious to all that is being bruited about him. Klack, however, seems to have aged over the weekend. Much of the bounce and boyishness have gone from his manner, and the greying strands in his hair seem somehow more prominent. I don't feel at all confident in him.

Dec. 6th

My final visit to Dr Klack. After six weeks of treatment I feel very much the same as I did when I started: not positively worse, perhaps, but decidedly no better. Klack, however, who has really bounced back since the Divine Light Mission announced that they would not even deign to refute the allegations against the Perfect Master, seems to know better. 'I'm really pleased with the way your body's responded,' he tells me. 'Real big changes have taken place since you came here first. But I want you to keep on when you get back home, find someone who'll give you advanced treatment like you've been getting here. Because if you keep on the way you were going before, then you won't last long. I want to see you write a few more books,' he adds engagingly. I will, Klack, I will. I watch him gazing at me like a ventriloquist at his dummy, and a right dummy I feel too. Why do I not tell him that

I'm fully aware that he's a charlatan? It's utterly humiliating to know that he's totally confident that I think he's marvellous. But for some reason – perhaps kindness of heart, perhaps venomous hypocrisy, but most likely both – I continue to smile and nod gratefully. Actually I'm already thinking about the refund I'm due for the three visits paid for in advance that I haven't been able to fit in. Klack goes to the cupboard and brings out some bottles of vitamin pills. 'I want you to take these away with you. Keep that nutrition going until you can get some treatment fixed up back home. Kathy'll work out your account before you leave.' He holds out his hand. 'Good luck, John. It's been great working with you.' 'Goodbye, Larry, it's been great being worked on.' When Kathy has totted up my account it turns out that the sum due to me corresponds almost exactly to the cost of my supply of vitamin pills. I receive a dime in change. I put it in my pocket and step out onto the sidewalk. It is a beautiful bright winter's day. I stroll down the boulevard, as happy as a king.